CANTATRIX SOPRANICA L.

Georges Perec
with Harry Mathews

Cantatrix sopranica L.

Scientific Papers

Introduced by Marcel Bénabou
Translations by Antony Melville,
Ian Monk & John Sturrock

ATLAS PRESS, LONDON, 2008

Published by Atlas Press,
27 Old Gloucester St., London WC1N 3XX.   .
Original edition *Cantatrix sopranica L.*, Éditions du Seuil, 1991.
©Éditions du Seuil, 1991
Collection La Librairie du XXIᵉ siècle, sous la direction de Maurice Olender
This edition ©2008, Atlas Press
All rights reserved.
Printed by Athenæum Press, Gateshead.
A CIP record for this book is available from
The British Library.
ISBN: 1 900565 48 X
ISBN-13: 978-1-900565-48-6

Contents

Marcel Bénabou

Introduction

Translated by Ian Monk

Parody, pastiche, satire or caricature? It is up to the reader to choose the term that best describes each of these texts, which reveal the sometimes neglected aspect of Perec the scholar.

Both taste and obligation led Georges Perec to examine the most varied disciplines, in which he always acquitted himself more as a connoisseur than an amateur.

Having adopted the ambitious project of trying his hand at all literary genres, he was soon drawn to the particularly charming idea of imitating scientific texts; the pleasure of possessing encyclopædic knowledge is thus united with the appeal of play, *trompe l'œil* and deception.

But Perec the parodist of course also retained characteristics of Perec the "serious" writer. Given his taste for exhaustiveness, he gradually explored all of the possibilities on offer. By turn, he became a neurophysiologist in order to report the results of an experiment on the effects of throwing tomatoes at divas, an entomologist so as to study the hybridisation of butterflies on the Isle of Iputupi, a hagiographer to celebrate the friendship between two great men, and a historian to present the Cathedral of Chartres. Finally, with his friend

Harry Mathews, he became an expert philologist in order to deliver an impeccable analysis of an unpublished text by Raymond Roussel, which is as mysterious as it is precious.

In Georges Perec's expert hands, this game takes on varied forms from one text to another, and adopts different registers. But the reader will soon discover the common point in them all: behind the accumulation of the external signs of scientific seriousness (maps, figures, diagrams, references, bibliographies and the frequent use of foreign languages) lies the endless shimmering of verbal play.

Georges Perec
Laboratoire de physiologie
Faculté de médecine Saint-Antoine
Paris, France

Experimental Demonstration of the Tomatotopic Organisation in the Soprano (*Cantatrix sopranica L.*)

In English originally

Abstract:

Experimental demonstration of a tomatopic organisation in Cantatrix sopranica L.

The author studies the ways in which tomato-throwing sets off the *yelling reaction* in the Chantatrix and shows how various areas of the brain are involved in the response, in particular the vegetal course, the thalamic nuclei and the lyrical fissure of the north hemisphere.

As observed at the turn of the century by Marks & Spencer (1899), who first named the "yelling reaction" (YR), the striking effects of tomato throwing on Sopranos have been extensively described. Although numerous behavioural (Zeeg & Puss, 1931; Roux & Combaluzier, 1932; Sinon *et al.*, 1948), pathological (Hun & Deu, 1960), comparative (Karybb & Szÿlâ, 1973) and follow-up (Else & Vire, 1974) studies have permitted a valuable description of these typical responses, neuro-anatomical, as well as neurophysiological data, are, in spite of their number, surprisingly confusing. In their henceforth late twenties' classical demonstrations, Chou & Lai (1927 *a, b, c*, 1928 *a, b*, 1929 *a*, 1930) have ruled out the hypothesis of a pure facio-facial nociceptive reflex that has been advanced for many years by a number of authors (Mace & Doyne, 1912; Payre & Tairnelle, 1916; Sornette & Billevayzé, 1925). Since that time, numerous observations have been made that have tried to decipher the tangling puzzle as well as the puzzling tangle of the afferent and/or efferent sides of the YR and led to the rather chaotic involvement of numberless structures and paths: trigeminal (Loewenstein *et al.*, 1930), bitrigeminal (Von Aitick, 1940), quadritrigeminal (Van der Deder, 1950), supra-, infra-, and inter-trigeminal (Mason & Rangoun, 1960) afferents have been likely pointed out as well as macular (Zakouski, 1954), saccular (Bortsch, 1955), utricular (Malosol, 1956), ventricular (Tarama, 1957), monocular (Zubrowska, 1958), binocular (Chachlik, 1959-1960), triocular (Strogonoff, 1960), auditive (Balalaïka, 1515) and digestive (Alka-Seltzer, 1815) inputs. Spinothalamic (Attou & Ratathou, 1974), rubrospinal (Maotz & Toung, 1973), nigro-striatal (Szentagothai, 1972), reticular (Pompeiano *et al.*, 1971), hypothalamic (Hubel & Wiesel, 1970), mesolimbic (Kuffler, 1969) and cerebellar (High & Low, 1968) pathways have been vainly searched out for a tentative explanation of the YR organisation and almost every part of the somaesthesic (Pericoloso & Sporgersi, 1973), motor (Ford, 1930), commissural (Gordon & Bogen, 1974) and associative (Einstein *et al.*, 1974) cortices have been found responsible for the progressive building-up of the response although, up to now, no decisive demonstration of both the input and output of the YR programming has been convincingly advanced.

Recent observations by Unsofort & Tchetera pointing out that *"the more you throw tomatoes on Sopranoes, the more they yell"* and comparative studies dealing with the gasp-reaction (Otis & Pifre, 1964), hiccup (Carpentier & Fialip, 1964), cat purring (Remmers & Gautier, 1972), HM reflex (Vincent *et al.*, 1976), ventriloquy (McCulloch *et al.*, 1964), shriek, scream, shrill and other hysterical reactions (Sturm & Drang, 1973) provoked by tomato as well as cabbages, apples, cream tarts, shoes, buts and anvil throwing (Harvar

& Mercy, 1973) have led to the steady assumption of a positive feedback organisation of the YR based upon a semilinear quadristable multi-switching interdigitation of neuronal subnetworks functioning *en désordre* (Beulott *et al.*, 1974). Although this hypothesis seems rather seductive, it lacks anatomical and physiological foundations and we therefore decide to explore systematically the internal incremental or decremental organisation of the YR, allowing a tentative anatomic model.

MATERIALS AND METHODS

Preparation

Experiments were carried out on 107 female healthy Sopranos (*Cantatrix sopranica L.*) furnished by the Conservatoire national de Musique, and weighing 94-124 kg (mean weight: 101 kg). Halothane anaesthesia was utilised during the course of tracheotomy, fixation in the Horsley-Clarke, and major operative procedures. 5% procaine was injected into skin margins and pressure points. Animals were then immobilised with gallamine triethyiodide (40 mg/kg/hr) and normocapnia was maintained by appropriate artificial ventilation. Spinal cord transections were performed at L^3/T^2 levels, thus eliminating blood pressure variations and adrenaline secretion induced by tomato throwing (Giscard d'Estaing, 1974). The fact that the animals were not suffering from pain was shown by their constant smiling throughout the experiments. Internal temperature was maintained at 38°C ± 4°F by means of three electrically-driven boiling kettles.

Stimulation

Tomatoes (*Tomato rungisia vulgaris*) were thrown by an automatic tomato-thrower (Wait & See, 1972) monitored by an all-purpose laboratory computer (DID/92/85/P/331) operated on-line. Repetitive throwing allowed up to 9 projections per sec, thus mimicking the physiological conditions encountered by Sopranos and other Singers on stage (Tebaldi, 1953). Care was taken to avoid missed projections on upper and/or lower limbs, trunk & buttocks. Only tomatoes affecting faces and necks were taken into account.

Control experiments were made with other projectiles, as apple cores, cabbage runts, hats, roses, pumpkins, bullets, and ketchup (Heinz, 1952).

Recording

Unit activity was recorded through glass-tungsten semi-macroelectrodes located *au-petit-bonheur*, according to the methods of Zyszytrakyczywsz-Sekrâwszkiwcz (1974). Spike recognition was performed by audio-monitoring: every time a unit discharge was heard, it was carefully photographed, tapped, displayed on a monograph and, after integration, on a polygraph. Statistical evaluation of the results was made using a tennis-like algorithm (Wimbledon, 1974), that is, every time a structure responds to win the game, it was recognised as YR-related.

Histology

At the end of the experiments, Sopranos were perfused with olive oil, and 10% Glenn Fiddish, and incubated at 421°C in 15% orange juice during 47 hours. Frozen 2 cm unstained sections were mounted into δ-strawberry sherbet and observed under light and heavy microscopy. Histological verifications confirmed that all the electrodes were located in the brain except four that were found in cauda equina and filum terminale and disclosed from statistical analysis.

RESULTS

Stereotaxic explorations of brains during tomato throwing showed that most of the areas respond differently to the tomaesthetic stimulation. As can be seen from TABLE ONE, where the results are summarised, three (3) distinct areas gave definite, unambiguous and

Regions	Tomatic stimulation					
	1/s	2/s	3/s	4/s	5/s	15/s
whole brain	0.0	0.0	4.2	0.6	0.7	000.1
raphe area	3.1	4.1	5.9	5.9	5.9	000.2
septum	± 1	67	875	121	000	π 3517
thalamus	2.2	$\sqrt{3}$	456	± 7	8.9	0.0001
NARTpl	456	+ 2	–4	§§	"2"	± 0.001
hypothalamus	± "3	1 & 2	41	S.G	121	many
hippocampus	1/2	3%	$\sqrt{\S7}$	?	<16	0,±±7
cereb. cortex	yes	< 55	nsp	$\left\{ {0 \atop 0} \right\}$	±∞	71 ± 70
scMS	~31	~65	>87	00+	$\frac{345}{\{4\{}$	a few
apTL	0.0	3.1	6.7	$\sqrt{4}$	–	56%
amygdala	+ 3	± 3	3.3	333	3	$\int 3.33$
N. poissy	→8	0.0	→1	12←	M/5	1+1= 2
N. Pesch	3§4	781	↑2	↓34	!	!!!!!
N. ruber	Δ51	???	$\sum_{4}^{3}$	$\int^{0}$	415	maybe

TABLE ONE. Differential responding of tomatic stimulation in the brain at different frequencies.

constant responses: the nucleus anterior reticularis thalami pars lateralis (NARTpl), or nucleus of Pesch (Pesch, 1876; Poissy, 1880; Jeanpace & Desmeyeurs, 1932), the anterior portion of the tractus leguminosus (apTL), lying 3.5 mm above the obex and 4 mm right of the tentorium and the dorsal part of the so-called "musical sulcus" (scMS) of the left hemisphere (Donen & Kelly, 1956). It is of interest to notice that, if the left hemisphere was kept for analysis, the right hemisphere was left.

Examples of responses obtained from these structures can be seen in figure 1 where temporal analysis of the spike distribution based on their Responsive-Area-Temporal-Programming (RATP) properties allowed to distinguish 3 unit subtypes: 1) units responding before the stimulation; 2) units responding during the stimulation and 3) units responding after the stimulation.

Cross-examination of responses driven by other projectiles and Ketchup stimulation are shown in figure 2 and argue unquestionably in favour of a tomatotopic organisation of the YR along, between and across the NARTpl, apTL and scMS. Temporal relationships of those responses, as exemplified in fig. 3, showed that the hypothesis of a clustering interdigitation of neuronal subnets is highly probable, although no experimental evidence can be given due to the relative difficulty of entering those damned structures without destroying a lot of things (Timeo et al., 1971).

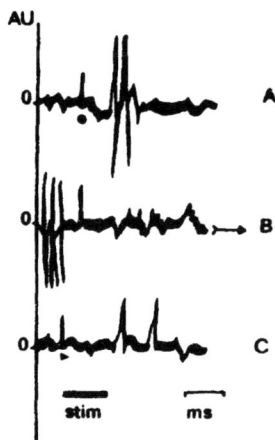

Fig. 1: Unit activity in structures responding to tomatic stimulation. Bar indicates stimulus onset & cessation. Calibration: 3.1416 ms. Each trace is made of the superimposition of 33.57 successive recordings. Note the point in A, the arrow in B and the black triangle in C.

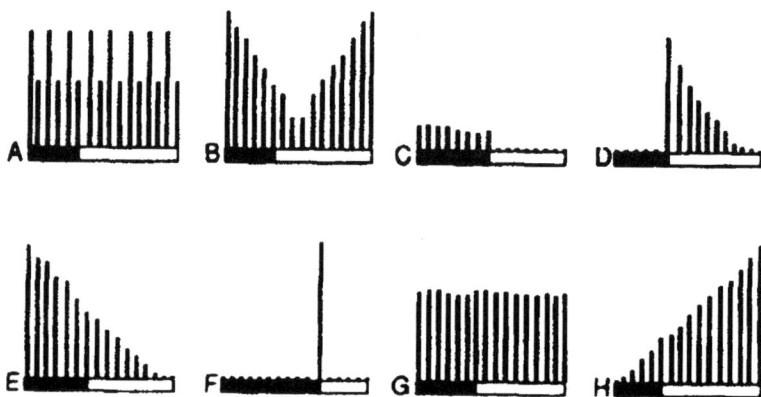

Fig. 2: Examples of responses in the apTL provoked by tomato and other throwings. Explanations in text.
A = tomato; B = apple; C = cabbage; D = hats; E = roses; F = ketchup*; G = pumpkin; H = bullet.
*Kindly provided by Laroche-Ciba, Inc.

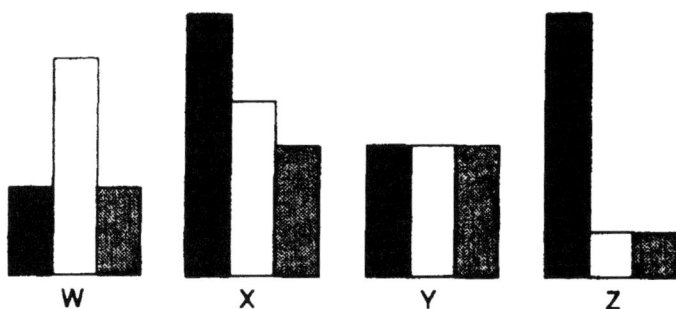

Fig. 3: Temporal relationships of the responses recorded in the YR area. Abscissae: arbitrary units; ordinates: international units. Explanation in text.

DISCUSSION

It has been shown above that tomato throwing provokes, along with a few other motor, visual, vegetative and behavioural reactions, neuronal responses in 3 distinctive brain areas: the nucleus anterior reticular thalami, pars lateralis (NARTpl), the anterior portion of the tractus leguminosus (apTL) and the dorsal part of the so-called musical sulcus (scMS). As pointed out by Chou & Lai (1929 *b*), Lai & Chou (1931 *a*, *b*) and Unsofort & Tchetera (1973), the YR organisation cannot be simply reduced to an oligosynaptic facio-facial nociceptive reflex which would have relayed over in the fascia leguminosa of the VIth laminations of the ventral quadrants of the paleospino-rubro-yello-tectocerebello-nigrostriatal tomatonergic ascending pathways. For the fact that horseradish peroxidase injected into the Sopranos' vocal chords is retrogradually transported from the apical dendrites of the vagus nerves to the tomato-tomatic synapses of the contralateral pseudo-gasserian afferents (McHulott *et al.*, 1975) proves with some likelihood the leguminous nature of the mediator responsible for the transmission of the message from the receptive tomato fields to the YR circuitry (Colle *et al.*, 1973). Thus, 3.5 (M-tri) argyril-p-*L*-tomatase which is selectively trisynthetised in the NARTpl-apTL bundle and whose destruction blocks up drastically the YR (Others *et al.*, 1974) stands out as the major candidate for the transmitter involved in the YR retroacting loop, although an alternate hypothesis based upon latency calculations, and cocross frequency correlations, puts forward the feasibility of a tomatotonic synapse (see Dendritt & Haxon, 1975). Although decisive experimental evidences are still lacking and further series of experiment are needed before the complete elucidation of the YR can be achieved, it seems logical to advance that above combined arguments along with experimental results described in our work are likely to support the hypothesis of a semi-linear multi-stable multi-switching net-back feed-work organisation of the YR whose tentative anatomical model can therefore be proposed (fig. 4).

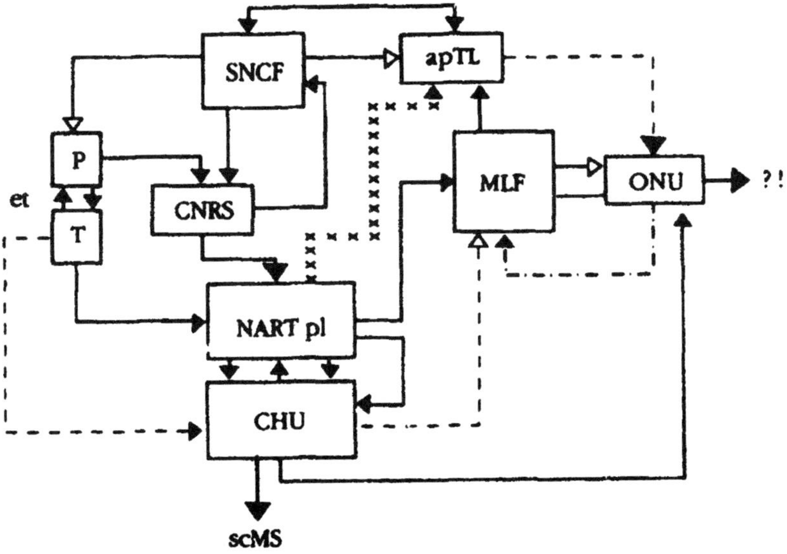

Fig. 4: Tentative anatomical model of the YR organisation. Explanations in text or elsewhere. Black lines = inhibitory; broken lines = interrogatory; dashed lines = redhibitory; stellate lines = whig-and-tory.

This work was supported by grants from the Syndicat régional des Producteurs de Fruits & Légumes, the Association française des Amateurs d'Art lyrique (AFAAL) and the Fédération internationale des Dactylo-Bibliographes (FIDB).

The author gratefully acknowledges the helpful criticisms as well as the skilful assistance of J. Chandelier, M. De Miroschedji and H. Gautier.

REFERENCES

Alka-Seltzer, L. *"Untersuchungen über die tomatostaltische Reflexe beim Walküre"*, Bayreuth *Monatschr. f. exp. Biol.* 184, 34-43, 1815.

Attou, J. & Ratathou, F. "Laminar configuration of the thalamo-tomatic relay nuclei. Experimental study with Fink-Heimer-Gygax methods." In: *The Hyperthalamus*, ed. V. Cointreau and M. Brizard, Cambridge, Oxford U.P., pp.32-88, 1974.

Balalaïka, P. "Deafness caused by tomato injury. Observations on half a case." *Acta pathol. marignan.* 1, 1-7, 1515.

Beulott, A., Rebeloth, B. & Dizdeudayre, C.D. *Brain Designing.* Chateauneuf-en-Thymerais, Institute of Advanced Studies (vol. 17), 1974.

Bortsch, B. "Saccular disturbances produced by whistling (in russian)." *Fortschr. Hals-Nasen-Ohrenheilk.* 3, 412-417, 1955.

Carpentier, H. & Fialip, L. "Tomato calibres & swallowing." *Bull. diet. gastrom. Physiol.* 3, 141-167, 1964.

Chachlik, I. "Vocal performance and binoculars." *Covent Gard. J.* 307, 1975-1980, 1959-1960.

Chou, O. & Lai, A. "Tomatic inhibition in the decerebrate baritone." *Proc. koning. Akad. Wiss., Amst.* 279, 33, 1927 *a*.

Chou, O. & Lai, A. "Note on the tomatic inhibition in the singing gorilla." *Acta laryngol.* 8, 41-42, 1927 *b*.

Chou, O. & Lai, A. "Further comments on inhibitory responses to tomato splitting in Soloists." *Z. f. Haendel Wiss.* 17, 75-80, 1927 c.

Chou, O. & Lai, A. "Faradic responses to tomatic stimulation in the buzzling ouistiti." *J. Amer. Metempsych. Soc.* 19, 100-120, 1928 *a*.

Chou, O. & Lai, A. "Charlotte's syndrome is *not* a withdrawal reflex. A reply to Roux & Combaluzier." *Folia pathol. musicol.* 7, 13-17, 1928 *b*.

Chou, O. & Lai, A. "Tomatic excitation and inhibition in awake Counteralts with discrete or massive brain lesions." *Acta chirurg. concertgebouw., Amst.* 17, 23-30, 1929 *a*.

Chou, O. & Lai, A. *"Musicali effetti del tomatino jettatura durante il reprezentazione dell' opere di Verdi.*" In: *Festschrift am Arturo Toscanini, herausgegeb. vom* A. Pick, I. Pick, E. Kohl & E. Gramm., München, Thieme & Becker, pp.145-172, 1929 *b.*

Chou, O. & Lai, A. "Suprasegmental contribution to the yelling reaction. Experiments with stimulation and destruction." *Ztschr. f. d. ges. Neur. u. Psychiat.* 130, 631-677, 1930.

Colle, E., Etahl, E. & Others, S. "Leguminase pathways in the brain. A new theory." *J. Neurochem. Neurocytol. Enzymol.* 1, 8-345, 1973.

Dendritt, A. & Haxon, B. "Synaptic contacts in the Lily Pons." *Brain Res.,* 1975 (*in the press*).

Donen, S. & Kelly, G. *Singing in the Brain.* Los Angeles, M.G.M. Inc. Press, 1956.

Einstein, Z., Zweistein, D., Dreistein, V., Vierstein, F. & St. Pierre, E. "Spatial integration in the temporal cortex." *Res. Proc. neurophysiol. Fanatic Soc.* 1, 45-52, 1974.

Else, K. & Vire, A. de. "45-years tomato throwing on amateur Singers." *New Records Ass. J.* 27, 37-38, 1974.

Ford, G. "Highways and pathways for motor control." *J. Pyramid. Soc.* 30, 30, 1930.

Giscard d'Estaing, V. *"Discours aux transporteurs routiers de Rungis."* C. r. Soc. fr. Tomatol. 422, 6, 1974.

Gorden, H.W. & Bogen, J.E. "Hemispheric lateralization of singing after intracarotid sodium amylobarbitone." *J. Neurol. Neurosurg. Psychiat.* 37, 727-738, 1974.

Harvar, D. & Mercy, B.C.P. "Reward and punishment in Olympic throwers." *Hammersmith J.* 134, 12-15, 1973.

Heinz, D. "Biological effects of ketchup splatching." *J. Food Cosmet. Ind.* 72, 42-62, 1952.

High, A.B.C.D. & Low, E.F.G.H. "Cerebellar aphonia and the Callas syndrome." *Brain* 91, 23-1, 1968.

Hubel, D.H. & Wiesel, T.N. "Receptive & tomato fields in the zona incerta." *Experientia* 25, 2, 1970.

Hun, O. & Deu, I. *Tonic, diatonic, & catatonic stage-distress syndromes.* Basel, Karger, 1960.

Jeanpace, L. & Desmeyeurs, P. *"Recherches histologiques sur les noyaux de Pesch & de Poissy." Dijon méd.* 5, 1-73, 1932.

Karybb, H. & Szÿlâ, H. "Of birds and men: calling strategies and humming responses." *Biol. Gaz. Elec.* 73, 19-73, 1973.

Kuffler, S.W. "Papezian control of aggressive borborygms in Julliard drop-out." *J. physiol. Physiol.* 2, 21-42, 1969.

Lai, A. & Chou, O. *"Dix-sept recettes faciles au chou et à l'ail. I. Avec des tomates." J. Ass. philharmon. Vet. lang. fr.* 3, 1-99, 1931 a.

Lai, A. & Chou, O. *"Dix-sept recettes faciles au chou et à l'ail. II. Avec d'autres tomates." J. Ass. philharmon. Vet. lang. fr.* 3, 100-1, 1931 b.

Loewenstein, W.R., Lowenfeld, I., Lövencraft, N., Løwoenshrift, Q. & Leuwwen, X. "Tomatic neuralgia." *J. Neurosurg. Psychiat. Neurol.* 340, 34-89, 1930.

Mace, I. & Doyne, J. *"Sur les différents types de réactions tomateuses chez la Cantatrice." Gaz. méd. franco-rus.* 6, 6-11, 1912.

Malosol, T. "Utricular responses during tomato conditioning." *Bull. méd. Aunis & Saintonge* 43, 6-11, 1956.

Maotz, E. & Toung, I. "Tomatic innervation of the nucleus ruber." *Proc. Opossum Soc.* 70, 717-727, 1973.

Marks, C.N.R.S. & Spencer, D.G.R.S.T. "About the frightening reactions that accompanied first performances of *Il Trovatore* at the Metropolitan." *Amer. J. Music. Deficiency* 7, 3-6, 1899.

Mason, H.W. & Rangoun, S.W. *"Paratrigeminaloid musicalgia."* In: *3rd Conference on the Rimsky-Korsakoff Syndrome*, ed. T. Thanos & P. Roxidase, Springfield, Ill., C.C. Thomate, pp.31-57, 1960.

McCulloch, W.S., Pitts, W.H. & Levin, R.D. Jr. "What the frog's stomach tells the frog's audience." *Proc. Leap & Frog Ass.* 64, 643-1201, 1964.

McHulott, E., Mac Haskett, E. & Massinture, E.T.C. "Fate of exogenous (^{14}C) scotch, (^{235}U) bloodymary and other tritiated compounds injected in laryngeal and pharyngeal pathways." *Clin. Bull. B.P.R. Soc.* 89, 35-78, 1975.

Others, S., Colle, E. & Etahl, E. "The enzymase enigma revisited." *Am. J. Allegrol.* 43, 234-567, 1974.

Otis, J. &. Pifre, K. "Gasping in the ascending pathways." In: *Hommage à Henri*

Eiffel, ed. D. Haux & D. Bas, Paris. C.N.R.S., pp.347-950, 1964.

Payre, L. & Tairnelle, E. "*Sur le sursaut tomateux du Baryton léger.*" *C.R. Assoc. Conc. Lam.* 45, 6-7, 1916.

Pericoloso, O. & Sporgersi, I. "*Sull' effetti tomestetiche e corticali della stimolazione di leguminose nella* Diva." *Arch. Physiol. Schola Cantor.* 37, 1805-1972, 1973.

Pesch, U. "*Experimentelle Beiträge über anterior reticularis Kerne beim Minnesänger.*" *Von Bulow's Arch. f. d. Ges. Musikol.* 1, 1-658, 1876.

Poissy, N. de. "*Atrophie congénitale des Noyaux de Pesch.*" *Bibl. clin. Homeoprat. Lugdun.* 65, 22-31, 1880.

Pompeiano, O., Vesuviana, A., Strombolino, H. & Lipari, G. "*Volcaniche effetti della formazione reticolare nella funiculi funicula.*" *C. r. Ass. ital. Amat. Bel Cant.* 37, 5-32, 1971.

Remmers, J.E. & Gauthier, H. "Neural and mechanical mechanisms of feline purring." *Respir. Physiol.* 16, 351-361, 1972.

Roux, C.F. & Combaluzier, H.U. "*Le syndrome de Charlotte.*" *Weimar Ztschr. musikol. Pomol.* 7, 1-14, 1932.

Sinon, E., Evero, I. & Ben Trovato, A. "Psycho-pathological description of *La Furia di Caruso* (in Italian)." *Folia clin. oto-rhinolaryngol., Foum Tataouine* 6, 362-363, 1948. (Quoted by Hun & Deu, 1960).

Sornette, U. & Billevayzé, H. "*Les stomatites tomateuses.*" *Arch. municip. Météorol. lyr. Déontol. music.* 264, 14-18, 1925.

Strogonoff, H., "III. Pineal activation and the yelling reaction." *Show Busin. med. Gaz.* 3, 273-308, 1960.

Sturm, U. & Drang, F. *Musikalische Katastrophe.* Berlin, W. de Gruyter, 1973.

Szentagothai, J. "The substantia nigra as a striatal machine." *Bull. Ass. niger. Neurophysiol. clin. exp., Niamey* 23, 25-40, 1972.

Tarama, K. *Acid-base balance.* PhD Thesis, San Francisco, 1957.

Tebaldi, R. "La Callas revisited." *Metropolitan J. Endocrin. Therap.* 6, 37-73, 1953.

Timeo, W., Danaos, I. & Dona-Ferentes, H.E.W. "Brain cutting and cooking." *Arch. metaphys. endogen. Gastrom.* 56, 98-105, 1971.

Unsofort, H. & Tchetera, K.G.B. "Shout and Yell." *Yale J. Med.* 9, 9-19, 1973.

Van der Deder, J. Von. "The yelling pathway." *San Diego J. Exp. Teratol.* 50, Suppl.

24, 1-28, 1950.

Vincent, J., Milâne, J., Danzunpré. J.J. & Sanvaing-Danlhotte, J.J.J. *"Le réflexe hydro-musical."* *Gaz. méd. Faidh. Chalign. & d.s. Fil.*, 1976 (*in the press*).

Von Aitick, A. *"Ueber geminal-niebelungenischen* Schmerz.*" Ztschr. exp. pathol. Tomatol.* 4, 4a-64P, 1940.

Wait, H. & See, C. "Ballistic requirements in tomato throwing and splatching." *Nasa Rept. No. 68/675/002/F4*, 1-472, 1972.

Wimbledon, A.F.G.H. "On the statistical matching of neuronal and other data." *J. Dynam. Stat.* 5, 1-28, 1974.

Zakouski, B.G.H. *"Investigations d'avant-garde sur les voies fluviales artificielles à moitié rondes dans le hall d'entrée (traduit du russe)."* *Exp. J. sechenov. Pflügerol.* 3, 17-34, 1954.

Zeeg, O. & Puss, I. K. "On the fanatic demonstrations of music lovers." *J. Behav. Developm. Psychobiol.* 31, 1-13, 1931.

Zubrowska, A. "Oculo-tomatic dyskinesia. A preliminary report." *J. Neuro-neurol. Neurol.* 1, 107, 1958.

Zyszytrakyczywsz-Sekrâwszkiwcz, I. "The Monte Carlo theorem as a use in locating brain and other sites." *J. Math. Vivisec.* 27, 134-143, 1974.

Pogy O'Brien
Department of Comparative Entomology
Fitchwinder University (Swetham, Mass., USA)

and Johann Wolfluss
Department of Mathematical Biology
University of Canberra (Australia)

The Spatio-Temporal Distribution of *Coscinoscera Victoria, Coscinoscera tigrata carpenteri, Coscinoscera punctata Barton & Coscinoscera nigrostriata* on the Island of Iputupi

Translated by Ian Monk

Abstract

Revisiting the Macklin data on a 3-year periodic cycle for *Coscinoscera Victoria* and hypothesising a relationship between crop destruction due to *hara'u* and presence of *Coscinoscera tigrata carpenteri* led us to reconstruct the spatio-temporal distribution of *Coscinoscera tigrata carpenteri* and consequently to predict locational and seasonal patterns of emergence of their hybrids *Coscinoscera punctata Barton* and *Coscinoscera nigrostriata*.

INTRODUCTION AND HISTORY

The first specimens of *Coscinoscera* were brought to London in 1902 by Barton on returning from his third journey to Melanesia (Barton, 1911). They were studied by Ludmer (1902) then by Illaca, Giacosa & Puccini (1904) thus allowing Pudatch (1905) to formulate the now commonly accepted principle of double hybridisation among the large Ornithoptera (Fig. 1).

Figure 1: The Hybridisation Principle of Coscinoscera
(according to Pudatch, 1905)

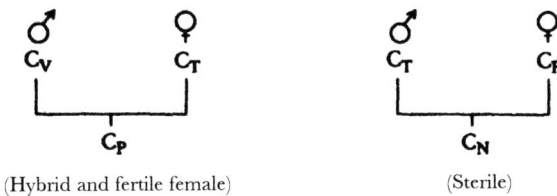

♂   ♀   ♂   ♀
C_V C_T C_T C_P

C_P C_N

(Hybrid and fertile female)   (Sterile)

However, it soon became clear that, while *Coscinoscera Victoria* (C_V) and *Coscinoscera tigrata carpenteri* (C_T) were widespread across all of the Solomon Islands, their hybrid varieties *Coscinoscera punctata* (C_P) and *Coscinoscera nigrostriata* (C_N) seemed to be present only on Iputupi, one of the smallest islands of the Louisiade archipelago, where Barton had had what seems to be the exceptional good fortune to capture some. In order to check the validity of his hypotheses and to try and specify the geographical and climatic conditions for the crossings C_V x C_T and C_T x C_P, Pudatch visited Amphlett and Misima in New Guinea in 1907, but his trip was a failure. A second expedition, organised in 1910 by Schmetterling Gesellschaft, was no more fortunate; a third, funded by the National Foundation for the Development of the Southern Hemisphere and led by Cervini, explored the Louisiade archipelago and the Entrecasteaux Islands systematically over a period of three years (1911-13) but still failed to procure any specimens of C_P or C_N. This research, interrupted by the First World War, was taken up again in the 1920s. But while the work of Macklin (1932) and Van Aargh (1938) made great strides in specifying the life conditions of C_V and C_T, nothing new was added concerning the two hybrid varieties, except that the probabilities of crossings between C_V and C_T (and *a fortiori* between C_T and C_P) seemed to be purely random. By the eve of the Second World War, most of the entomologists and geneticists who had paid any attention to the double hybridisation of *Coscinoscera* had abandoned their research, under the assumption that C_P and C_N were mere aberrant sub-varieties. However, a second specimen of C_N, which was indisputably authentic but of uncertain provenance, had been sold in

Singapore in 1928 to the American collector Seaward Blackmaster. Then, in 1933, the Australian Lieutenant Palmerston brought back 17 fine specimens of C_P from Iputitupi.

In 1965, the discovery of 45 specimens of C_P (Hayes, 1966) coincided with renewed interest in the problem of double hybridisation, other examples of which had just been located in Amazonia (Ehrlich, 1962) and in the New Hybrids (Nabokoff, 1964). In 1973, the South-East Asian Institute of Comparative Lepidoptery undertook an inventory of large Ornithoptera of the Solomon Sea and entrusted us with the district of the Calvados Islands (Panawine, Sabari, Hemenaei, Panatinani (Jeannet Island), Iputipitupi, Maturina and Menãbataho). It was when analysing the results obtained during the fieldwork of this research that we were led to examine the problem of double hybridisation of C_V and C_T, while taking into account recent progress made in the field of population dynamics.

RESULTS AND DISCUSSION

The fieldwork, carried out using techniques recently perfected by Stropovitch (1967) and Charrière (1971), confirmed the observations already made concerning C_V and C_T by Macklin and Van Aargh. Although classically grouped together in the same family, the two varieties belong to different ecosystems. While C_V seems to be a stable species mostly adopting type K bionomic strategies (May, 1971) (a population varying little in terms of its balance, longevity and optimum use of the environment), C_T on the other hand generally displays most of the particularities of type r strategies (Barclay, 1975) (a high level of fertility, sharp rises in the population, a rapid exhaustion of environmental resources and a territorial instability which is costly for the entire population). Population surveys in 1974-75 (fig. 2) clearly show the difference of habitat of the two varieties:

Figure 2: Territorial distribution of C_V and C_T

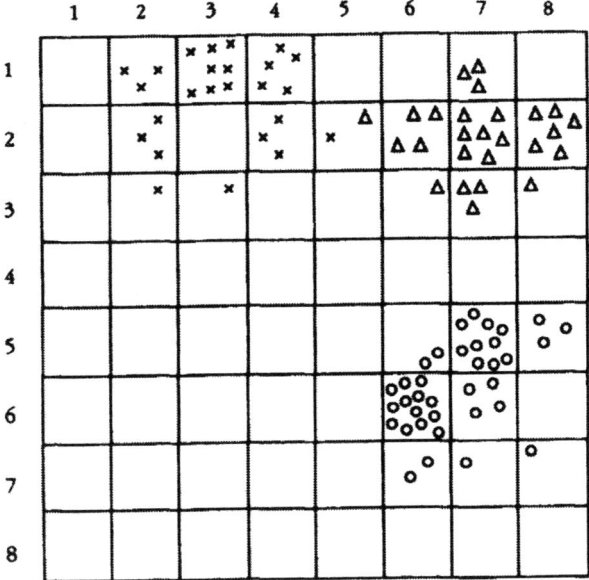

o C_V (1974-1975)   × C_T (1974)   ▲ C_T (1975)

Each point corresponds to 10 specimens.

C_V is essentially settled in the plain valley of the Black River;

C_T, on the other hand, is characterised by marked spatial and temporal variations. This territorial disparity posed once again the problem of contact between the two varieties: no specimen of C_P was found, neither in the zone discovered by Hayes in 1965 nor elsewhere, nor any specimens of C_N either.

As early as 1932, Macklin, who had been able to observe the behaviour of C_V over a ten-year period on the Isle of Buka (Solomon), could show that the density of the population grew regularly every three years, with the peak of the cycle corresponding to a clear upward shift of their usual group habitat, which rose from an altitude of 600-650 m to 650-680 m (fig. 3).

Fig. 3: Illustration of a three-year cycle among C_V on the Isle of Buka (according to Macklin, 1932)

Number of C_V found above 650 m.

It was thus reasonable to suppose that the C_V of Iputipupitupi had a similar cycle and that crossings of C_V x C_T occurred during peaks in this cycle when a clear excess in the male population led to them moving up the sides of the Black River valley in search of C_T females. But it was still necessary to prove that specimens of C_T inhabited the immediate vicinity of the C_V zone at that time.

Based on the slim experimental observations available (fig. 2), we supposed that C_T had a migratory behaviour that followed a cycle depending on the possibility for its caterpillars to feed. This hypothesis had already been formed by Van Aargh, who had noticed that the presence of C_T coincided with the appearance of *bara'u* (rhizome gangrene) in the yam fields. This type of behaviour corresponds closely to the theoretical behavioural type of populations following strategy *r*, as described by Southwood (1962) among the rhinopods: every two generations, the population exhausts the resources of its environment, explodes and moves to a different region; the first generation is extremely weak because of this exodus and builds itself back up thanks to its new environment, which it ravages systematically; the second generation is strong, but cannot feed and so is obliged to migrate.

We thus deduced a possible migratory circuit of C_T based on cases of *bara'u* observed in the yam fields of Iputiputupitupi. An examination of the archives of the Australian Authority for Agronomical Advancement (AAAA), which are unfortunately rather incomplete, confirmed this hypothesis and showed that C_T follows an eight-year cycle, passing through the four main yam-growing regions on the island (see Map 1 overleaf and Table I).

Table I: Theoretical temporal distribution of C_T in the four main yam-growing regions

Zone 1	Zone 2	Zone 3	Zone 4
1899 1900	1901 1902	1903 1904	1905 1906
1907 1908	1909 1910	1911 1912	1913 1914
1915 1916	1917 1918	1919 1920	1921 1922
1923 1924	1925 1926	1927 1928	1929 1930
1931 1932	1933 1934	1935 1936	1937 1938
1939 1940	1941 1942	1943 1944	1945 1946
1947 1948	1949 1950	1951 1952	1953 1954
1955 1956	1957 1958	1959 1960	1961 1962
1963 1964	1965 1966	1967 1968	1969 1970
1971 1972	1973 1974	1975	

The underlined years correspond to cases of *bara'u* in the zone in question.

The appearance of the hybrid C_P thus depends on:

1) the presence of C_T in zone 1;

2) the cycle of C_V.

Experimental data show that $C_V \times C_T$ crossings could have occurred in 1900, 1932 and 1964 (corresponding to the adult specimens gathered respectively by Barton, Palmerston and Hayes in 1901, 1933 and 1965). But while this schema does correspond to our

ISLAND OF IPUTUPI
Louisiade Archipelago

N

12°

152 E.

12"

Urania Cove

Mount Cabera

Cosmia Point

Marshland

1911
3
1975
1951   1959
1968   1966
1967

1953
1913
4   1954
1946   1969
1970
1914   1929

1974
2   1965
1966   1933
1957

1955
1   1932
1956   1972
1971

1965
1973   1926
B   1958
1963

Black River Valley

Black River

Melo River

Cerepu River

A

1965

Mount Kokoma

Carpenter Bay

Melitié

Chocho Point

Fidonia

Rh'a Point

0   1 km

38

Key to Map 1: The Isle of Iputupi

C_V Zone: from 600 to 650 m

C_V Zone at peak of cycle: between 650 and 680 m

C_T Zones

Direction of circuit

[1965] Confirmed cases of *bara'u*

A and **B** C_P habitats

(Inset map (Map 2) is on p.42 below)

theoretical model for the circuit of C_T, it is incompatible with the three-year cycle of C_V as proposed by Macklin. Table II shows clearly that, whatever temporal base is chosen, it only functions for itself and excludes the other two.

Table II: Illustration of the contradiction between
Macklin's cycle and the appearance of C_P

C_V	3-year cycle	0	3	6	9	12	15	18	21	24	27	30	33	36
		2	5	8	11	14	17	20	23	26	29	32	35	
	Inter-cycle years	1	4	7	10	13	16	19	22	25	28	31	34	
C_T	Presence in zone 1	×		× ×		× ×			× ×			×	×	
		B											P		

39	42	45	48	51	54	57	60	63	66	69	72	75
38	41	44	47	50	53	56	59	62	65	68	71	74
37	40	43	46	49	52	55	58	61	64	67	70	73
× ×		× ×		× ×			×	×			× ×	
								H				

0 represents the year 1900, and 3 the year 1903, etc.
B, H and P represent the specimens found respectively by Barton, Hayes and Palmerston.

However, it has been known since Shelford (1943) that the dynamic of a population follows cycles that such periodic models do not always describe accurately, in that these cycles can run late or else jump forwards, in such a way that an entire passage can disappear. The application of an equation of discrete delay ($rT = 2.4$) to our model introduces a slowdown every four years and allows our hypothesis to fit with all the experimental data (Table III).

Table III: Compatibility between a cyclical model with a delay for C_V and the experimental data

Cycle of C_V	0	3	6	9	12	16	19	22	25	28	32	35	38	41	44	48	51	54	57	60	64	etc.
Presence of C_T in zone 1	0			8		16			24		32			40		48			56		64	
	B										P										H	

B, H and P represent the specimens found respectively by Barton, Hayes and Palmerston.
NB: the years when there were probably appearances of uncaptured C_P are surrounded by dotted lines.

The fact that C_T and C_V coincide every sixteen years explains the rare appearances of C_P. But it can still be asked why each appearance of C_P is not accompanied, in the next generation, by an appearance of C_N, as was the case for the specimen found by Barton during his second journey to Iputiputitupitupi. For the migratory system of C_T should, as for C_P, determine the place and date of appearance of C_N:

1. Occurrence periods of C_P coincide with the passage of C_T from zone 1 to zone 2; it is thus on the migratory path of C_T from zone 1 to zone 2, or on the borders of zone 2, that C_T X C_P crossings can occur.

2. It has been known since Hayes that C_P, chased from its native territory by C_V, migrates within a limited perimeter and prefers to establish its habitat in a moist, non-marshy sector.

3. From localisation A, as given by Hayes, and using aerodynamic equations for *Lepidoptera* (Diamond, 1973), we have

described the possible perimeter of the migration of C_P. Within this perimeter, there are just two zones that correspond to the preferences of C_P: the first, Hayes' zone A, has no common point with C_T zones, but is closer to the birth territory of C_P and thus probably preferential; the second zone (B) only intersects with the migratory path of C_T between zones 1 and 2 in a highly limited area (see Map 2).

Map 2: Potential sites for the double hybridisation of C_P x C_T
(enlarged inset section of the main map)

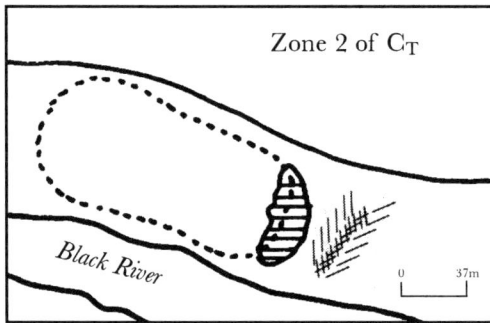

Zone 2 of C_T

Black River

0   37m

  Migratory path of C_T
(the density of the lines corresponds
to the frequency of passage)

  Perimeter limit of the habitat of C_P

  Fringe area with occurence of C_N
(70 x 10 m)

42

It can be supposed that zone B is chosen by C_P only when climatic and/or meteorological conditions forbid access to zone A, as was presumably the case in 1901 (Barton) and perhaps in 1928 (Seaward Blackmaster's specimen).

It is, in any case, only in this narrow fringe just a few metres wide that in May/June 1981 it may be possible to gather, in caterpillar or chrysalis form, some fresh specimens of C_N and thus solve once and for all the enigma of the double hybridisation of *Coscinoscera*.

NOTE: while this article was in the press, the AAAA carried out a large-scale extermination of C_T, at the time localised in zone 4.

This work was funded by the International Foundation for Entomological Heritage Protection and received a subsidy from the Australian Authority for Agronomical Advancement (AAAA), Canberra.

This article was originally published in Proceedings of the Butterfly Society of Australia *(1978, 17: 17-25) and was translated by Georges Perec in collaboration with Sylvia Lamblin-Richardson.*

REFERENCES

Barclay, H. "Population strategies and random environments." *Can. J. Zool.*, 1975, 55: 160-165.

Barton, F. *Wandering in the South Seas*, London, Methuen, 1911.

Charrière, I. "On measuring niche width." In: *Methods in Ecological Entomology*, ed. J.H. Benson, Oxford U.P., 1971.

Diamond, J.M. "Strategic aerodynamics and distributional ecology of New-Guinea butterflies." *Science*, 1973, 179: 759-769.

Ehrlich, P. "Models of hybridization in Heliconia." *Biotropica*, 1962, 1: 43-47.

Hayes, R. *The Fauna and Flora of the Calvados Islands.* Techn. Rept. of the AAAA, vol. 117, 1966: 1-198.

Illaca, G., Giacosa, F. & Puccini, G. "*Nouvelles hypothèses sur l'hybridation de Coscinoscera.*" *Rev. fr. Entomol.*, 1904, 17: 181-198.

Ludmer, V. "Phylogenetic considerations on Barton's butterflies." *Nature*, 1902, 97: 1897.

Macklin, C. "Longitudinal studies of *Coscinoscera Victoria* in Solomon Islands." *Tropicana*, 1932, 28: 192-403.

May, R.M. "Stability in model ecosystems." *Proc. Ecol. Soc. Austr.*, 1971, 6: 18-56.

Nabokoff, T. "Variety vs. rarity: the Simpsimus dilemma in Aurora Island." *Proc. Natl. Acad. Sci.*, 1964, 346: 432-435.

Pudatch, A. "*Doppel-Zwittergeschlechtes bei Ornithoptera.*" *Z. f. Entomol.*, 1905, 83: 114-142.

Shelford, V.E. "The relation of snowy owl migration to the abundance of collared lemming." *Auk*, 1943, 62: 592-594.

Southwood, T.R.E. "Migration of terrestrial Rhinopods in relation to habitat." *Biol. Rev.*, 1962, 37: 171-214.

Stropovitch, K. "Stochastic sampling as a methodological tool in population mathematics." *Biometrika*, 1967, 55: 228-232.

Van Aargh, G. "Territoriality in *Coscinoscera tigrata*. Facts and hypotheses." *Biol. Bull.*, 1938, 83: 120-133.

A Scientific and Literary Friendship: Léon Burp and Marcel Gotlib

followed by

Further Reflections on the Life and Work of Romuald Saint-Sohaint

Translated by John Sturrock

The recent award of the Nobel Prize for Experimental Botany to Marcel Gotlib, his triumphant election to the Lille-Roubaix-Tourcoing Academy of Sciences and his appointment as Plenipotentiary Counsellor for Social, Scientific and Cultural Affairs to the European Assembly, are concrete proof of the unanimously high esteem in which, for a number of years, the life's work of this indefatigable researcher has been held, who in the course of his dazzling career has, with an equal genius, blown wide open the major problem areas of contemporary science in most of the key disciplines, from group dynamics to quantum theory, from rural sociology to prehistoric musicology and from cellular anthropology to combinatory physiology. Receiving him last Friday beneath the Cupola,* Leprince-Ringuet was right when he said:

You have been able to give a decisive impulsion to researches which had previously been wallowing in error and mediocrity. You have been able to resolve, with a matchless elegance and virtuosity, the greater number of those painful enigmas in which generations of researchers had continued to be ensnared. You have been able

*I.e. into the Académie Française, meeting in its domed chamber. [Translator's notes are indicated by an asterisk.]

to clear the way that will soon lead us to the kingdom of Knowledge, to the knowledge of the Great Whole, to Man's decisive domination of an opaque and darkling Universe. Like a Democritus, a Newton, a Pasteur, a Valéry, a Radot, you have caused Science to accomplish the Great Leap Forward that will bring it out from the abyss on the brink of which it had been teetering.[1]

However, although the work of Marcel Gotlib is today universally known and acknowledged, and although most of his contributions have been amply disseminated and vulgarized by his historiographers and exegetes, one of the sectors in which his prodigious spirit of analysis and synthesis has shown itself with the greatest *éclat* has remained oddly in the shadows. Whereas the precious commentaries of Bouldu,[2] Lévi-Strauss,[3] Reiser,[4] Glützenbaum,[5] Ladding,[6] Oumboulélé,[7] Cloutier,[8] Slowburn,[9]

1. Leprince-Ringuet, L., *Comic Rays*, Paris, PUF, 1979.
2. Bouldu, I., "On the Use of Close Combat in the Detection of Deafness", *Arch. Criminol. Didact.*, 1972, 36, 47-58.
3. Lévi-Strauss, C., "The Myth of the Fish in Breton Folklore from Saint-Goménolé", *Rev. fr. Ethnol. compar.*, 1973, 143, 221-347.
4. Reiser, J.M., "*Untersuchen über Gotlib's Unterschrift des Ludwig Van's Pastorale*", *Z. f. Musikol. u. Akustik*, 1971, 63, 48-57.
5. Glützenbaum, O., "Gotlib's methods in acupunctural treatment of aerophagia", *Canad. J. Allergol.*, 1979, 3, 367-369.
6. Ladding, A., "Gotlib's contributions to the problem of street sanitation and garbage-can cleaning", *Brit. J. Soc. Hygiene*, 1976, 327, 1-45.
7. Oumboulélé, M., "*Ng'otlib ng'ifé m'purien ng'kadé m'siné m'dezizi*", *Nx. Ng'Cah. Ng'Folk. Afr.*, 1977, 48, 123-456.

Howland,[10] Druillet,[11] and Paul[12] have brought out once and for all the primordial role played by Gotlib in the fields of comparative criminology, structural anthropology, analytical musicology, clinical stomatology, urban sociology, African ethnology, descriptive geometry, genetic epistemology, integral statistics, political economy and molecular chemistry, nothing, or next to nothing, has been said concerning the prodigious series of experiments realised by Gotlib in the laboratory of Professor Burp between 1957 and 1963, which were so profoundly to overturn our knowledge in the fields of dynamic ethology and animal physiology. No doubt the tragic departure of Léon Burp and the painful silence which Marcel Gotlib imposed on himself for almost fifteen years explain why, out of all his researches, it is these that should have been the most reluctantly given to be known by the public at large. But the time has come today to lift the veil on this unique and exemplary collaboration which will forever remain a model for all researchers. The publication of the

10. Howland, D., "Gotlibian Measurements in Bantu Statuary. Theory and Methods", *Bull. Archeol. quantit.*, 1969, 3, 56-80.
11. Druillet, P., "Capitalist Economy and Tax Credits", *Sem. Zézet.*, 1978, 45, 1165-7.
12. Paul, P., "On the Presence of Cannabinol in Lyophilized Broccoli", *Quart. Bull. Police Lab.*, 1979, 158, 975-1007.

8. Cloutier, R., "Gotlib's Equations Applied to the Calculation of Prespherical, Volumes", *Arch. Int. Mathemat. Transcend.*, 1976, 66, 34-36.
9. Slowburn, J.L., "*Varietti effetti della rigoladda nelle duellistti*", *Arch. Ital. Rigol. Zigomatol*, 1975, 99, 198-246.

correspondence which the two men kept up between 1954 and 1963,[13] finally authorised by Marcel Gotlib, shows very clearly that it is now time to reveal to the scientific world the extraordinary results that they achieved.

Léon Burp and Marcel Gotlib had been friends from the very start. They were both born in Vaudouhé-lès-Gonesse and Léon's uncle's godmother's son was the second cousin of Marcel's sister, Liliane's, husband's nephew. They were fellow pupils at the Great Swiss Seminary in Roubaix, as well as fellow members of the choral group, the "Joyful Nightingales of the Côtes-du-Rhône". Then their destinies grew apart. While Marcel Gotlib, with the talents of which we already know, launched himself on a career as a theatre director (these were the days of *Tragic Picnic*, *Stockbreeding in Burgundy*, *Five Foot Six* and *The Gendarme Goes into Retirement*), Léon Burp, after having worked for a while as an expert in macaronic spaghettology in the laboratories of Félix Potin,* left for Austria to sit at the feet of Von Glütenschtummelhimdörf.

For a number of years, the two men met only on special occasions, such as the wedding of Ferdinand Gotlib, one of Marcel's cousins, in Vaudouhé (where he married Mlle F. Lacruche), or his uncle Philibert's reception into the Académie Française.[14]

---

13. Gotlib, M. and Burp, L., *Correspondance*, Louvain, Desclée de Brouwer, 1980, 17 vols.

*A chain of food shops in France. [Trans.]

It was now that Marcel Gotlib, discouraged by the commercial failure of his most ambitious work, *2002: A Space Odyssey*,[15] finally renounced the Seventh Art, symbolically setting fire in front of the terrace at Fouquet's to the scripts of the three films he was then planning, the titles alone of which have come down to us: *The Things of the Life Ahead*, *Two Englishwomen and the Lost Continent* and *Balzac 001 versus Dr. No*. In fact it was at this time that Marcel Gotlib was to discover Leonardo da Vintchi and to realise that his true vocation was not the cinema but music.

Appointed the following week to be the head of the Metropolitan Opera in New York, he was to create there, in the course of the months that followed, some of the most notable works of those years: *The Blood-red Radiator Plug*, with Kurt Schtimmel, Hans Trüden, Klaus Ziegel, Wolfgang Gröbz and Magda Schweinhund, *Gault and Millau in the Far West*,* *Who is that Son of a Bitch Who Put Some*

---

15. The film was on the way to completion when there appeared on Parisian screens the gross forgery which Stanley Kubrick had knocked up in a few weeks. Gotlib's distributors and producers immediately broke off the filming, preferring to lose the six million dollars they had already invested rather than incur a certain catastrophe.

*Gault and Millau are the compilers of a highly regarded guide to French restaurants. [Trans.]

---

14. ...where he was appointed porter in replacement of M. Norbert Leglandu, who was allowed to exercise his right to retirement and took advantage of it to set up, along with his two great grand-daughters, a group of tap-dancers, the Three Klaps.

Soap in my Scotch?, magisterially interpreted by Ephraïm Zimbalist Jr., and *The Law of Gravitation*, a monumental saga retracing the prodigious life of Isaac Newton, which was to have a decisive influence on his subsequent changes of direction. But here too, the cabals and machinations hatched by the timorous spirits exasperated by the extent of his ambitions got the better of his tenacity. When he had the brilliant idea of having the eureka-style apple played by the young Zurich tenor Hans Spatenberg, the SPITIM (Society for the Protection of Individuals of a Tallness Inferior to the Mean) launched a series of demonstrations which led to the Opera House being closed.

Marcel Gotlib returned to France and went through a spiritual crisis in the course of which, assailed by doubts, he contemplated for a while going home to work in his father's coal merchant's business. But his appetite for knowledge, his intellectual curiosity and his unquenchable love of risk soon became uppermost again. It was now that, through the agency of the Chaprot family, of which they had both been long-standing intimates, he met up with Léon Burp once more, who, after having been the head accountant with Aristidès, the butcher and poulterer, had just started as head of research in the Laboratory of Comparative Animalology in the Department of Tropical Biology at Malaga-Saint-Ouen.

The rest we know. Within six years the collaboration of Burp and Gotlib had given rise to a series of articles in which all the problems that the specialists in animal physiology had been trying in vain for decades to resolve were elucidated one by one. It would be tedious to draw up the list of all these discoveries, so we shall content ourselves with recalling the most celebrated:

demonstration of the mimetic and ventriloquial faculties of the sloth[16]

discovery of neurotic behaviour patterns in certain animals disturbed by the human environment[17]

elucidation of the mysteries of pigmentation in the zebra[18]

explanation of dehydration in the camel[19]

analysis of the influence of the aquatic behaviour of the hippopotamus on river levels[20]

study of the speed of propagation of the nervous influx in the giraffe[21]

16. Burp, L. and Gotlib, M., "Observations on the Mimetic Behaviour of the Bradypus", *J. Physiol. Paris*, 1958, 47, 222.
17. Gotlib, M. and Burp, L., "On the Degradation of the Ego in Domestic Animals", *Arch. Psychiat. Animal.*, 1958, 66, 35-58.
18. Gotlib, M., Nioutonne, I. and Burp, L., "Topological Remarks on the Spatio-Temporal Modifications of the Zebra's Stripes (*Zebra zebra L.*)", *Bull. Physiopathol. Tropic.*, 1959, 47, 128-149.
19. Burp, L. and Gotlib, M., "Fluid Dynamics in *Chamelopsis sahariensis*". In: *The Fauna and Flora of Desert or Near Desert Climates*, H. Quatre, ed., Presses Universitaires de Brie et de Touraine, 1959, 236pp.
20. Gotlib, M., Oumboulélé, M. and Burp, L., "Note on the Use of *Porcinus artiodactylis hippopotamus* for Irrigation on the Banks of the Nile", *Z. f. Nilpferd. Wiss.*, 1959, 99, 375-387.

discovery of sub-tension in the pig[22]

experimental demonstration of stiffness in the pointer[23]

analysis of certain sexual behaviour patterns in the rabbit[24]

demonstration of ticklish zones in a normal human being[25]

and finally, their last two pieces of work, which turned the still primitive discipline of prehistoric anatomo-physiology upside down: one on the evolution of species and the appearance of the crocodile,[26] the other on the adhesive properties of the fossil snail.[27]

Léon Burp's departure, in the dramatic circumstances that we all know of, put a brutal stop to this collaboration, unique in the

22. Gotlib, M. and Burp, L., *"Ladespannung beim Schweine"*, *Arch. Wurstwar. u. Delikatess.*, 1960, 21, 635-723.

23. Burp, L. and Gotlib, M., "Stiffness and Ankylosis in Ground-game Dogs", *Science*, 1961, 145, 89-93.

24. Gotlib, M. and Burp, L., "Sexual Anomalies in the Rabbit", *Science*, 1961, 145, 93-97.

25. Burp, L., Blondeaux, G.J.B., Raffray, X. and Gotlib, M., "Zygomatic Reflexes and Ticklish Zones". In: *International Colloquium on Desopilating Characters and their Effects on Humans*, M. Greg, J. Bonessian, A. Glützenbaum and M. Gotlib eds., Oxford U. P., 1961, 345-576.

26. Gotlib, M. and Burp, L., "Phylogenetic Considerations on the Crocodile. Facts and Hypotheses", *J. Palaeontol. Embryol.*, 1962, 1, 23-89.

27. Burp, L. and Gotlib, M., "Vorgeschichtliche Biologie des Schneckes" In: *Studies in Palaeophysiology* Vol. 1, Heidelberg, 1963.

21. Burp, L., Gotlib, M. and Burp, L., "Latency of the Reflex Arc in *Girafus girafo*", *Animal Studies*, 1960, 55, 356-387.

annals of science. Marcel Gotlib was approached by the Ministry for Scientific Research as Applied to Industry to replace his friend as head of the Laboratory of Comparative Animalology, but he refused, preferring to resume once more the arduous path of creation in grief, solitude and doubt.

Postscript: New Reflections on the Life and Work of Romuald Saint-Sohaint

On several occasions in his works, Marcel Gotlib makes reference to an obscure man of science of whom history has not even retained the name but to whom we owe the paper-clip, the press-stud and the edible boomerang. Our own researches having led us into neighbouring domains, we became keen to learn more about this unacknowledged inventor, whose name at least it seems inconceivable has not been somewhere preserved; and everything gives us to think that the man in question can only be Romuald Saint-Sohaint.

Romuald Saint-Sohaint was born in 1802 in Besançon. His father, Nicolas Saint-Sohaint, was the orderly of General the Count Hugo, who much esteemed his great valour and great size and, very often, on the evening after a battle, took him with him to ride on horseback across the field strewn with the dead on whom the darkness was falling. Everything gives us to suppose that the young Romuald had for the companion of his childhood games the young Victor Hugo, but nothing authorises us to assert that this left any particular mark on him. We know on the other hand that he revealed very early on an aptitude for algebra, geometry and physics. He entered the École Polytechnique at the age of twenty and left it at the age of twenty-four as a lieutenant of artillery. But garrison life no doubt failed to live up to his deepest aspirations for he resigned three years later. In 1830, in the salon of Mme Récamier at L'Abbaye-aux-Bois, he met a wealthy Spanish widow, the Countess d'Aguada, whom he married the following year. Freed henceforth from all financial worries, Saint-Sohaint was now able to devote himself entirely to his researches. In addition to the metal attachment known as the "paper-clip" (patented in 1847), the press-stud (patented in 1852, and recognised as being of public utility posthumously, in 1871), Saint-Sohaint discovered the principle of the liquefaction of methane, gamma particles, the origin of Hercynian folds, and the proof by nine,* which was rapidly disseminated among schools of every denomination and earned him the Academic Palms** in 1863. To him we also owe an automatic corkscrew based on guncotton, the sale of which was banned after the blaze in the canteen of the French Legation in Bucharest, a process for making paper at once softer and more resistant which was later taken up by Wolfgang Amadeus Quincampoix, a tricycle that could be completely dismantled, of

* A method taught in French schools of checking multiplication and division sums.
** Decoration dating back to 1808 and given for meritorious contributions to teaching and to the arts. Holders are entitled to wear a violet ribbon in their buttonhole.

which the postal authorities ordered 4,000, a system for holding up socks which was all the rage up until the beginning of this century, and a treatise in four volumes devoted to the surfacing and upkeep of local roads, for which he received the Prix Cabrisseau. But his most popular inventions, still in common use today, remain the screwdriver, the serving trolley, the rocking-chair, the nutcracker and the twist drill. And it was because he spent the last years of his life, from 1864 to 1868, in the Charenton Asylum, that the expressions "to have a screw loose", "to be off his trolley", "to be off his rocker", "to be crackers", and "to be round the twist" have for us the sense they do.

Nowhere in Saint-Sohaint's works have we found any trace of researches concerning a so-called "boomerang" custard-pie capable of returning to its starting-point once it has missed its target. On the other hand, Saint-Sohaint appears to have devoted his last moments of lucidity to perfecting a pie that would never miss its target and which, for reasons that remain obscure, he called the *"tarte des Demoiselles"*. It was no part of our purpose to ask ourselves what the reasons may have been which led Marcel Gotlib, whose erudition was customarily impeccable and without flaw, not to cite this man of science, unrecognised it is true but not truly unknown since a street in the 13th *arrondissement* still bears his name. It was in any case of interest, we thought, to dwell for a moment on this personage, nearly all of whose inventions and discoveries continue to play a part in our everyday lives.

Presentation:

From La Beauce to
Notre-Dame de Chartres

Translated by Ian Monk

Many generations of geographers and linguists have, for good reason, wondered about the toponymic origins of La Beauce: why should this large plateau — whose main characteristic is of course its *flatness* — have a name which in fact evokes relief, or at least protuberance? Etymology confirms but does not explain this connection: *Beauce* just like "embossed" or *bosse* (hump), *bossoir* (cathead of an anchor), *bossu* (hunchback) or the name "Bossuet", comes from the ancient Carnute root *'bos* meaning "elevation, swelling, nipple, puffing, eminence, roundness, summit, etc."; it may even be found in "Booz" as well as in the Medieval expression *"faire bosse neuve"*, describing the superstition of touching a hunchback's hump for good luck; finally, and more recently, it has returned in partial form to our shores after a long linguistic journey in the name of a typical dance originating from Brazil.

One of the strengths of Barandard's approach is that it attacks the problem head-on, instead of avoiding it, as has been the case previously for a large number of archaeologists, medievalists, architects, traffic specialists, ecologists, industrial-drawing teachers, oyster openers and what have you. Barandard even dares to declare out loud what everyone else had been thinking to themselves, while not daring to speak their minds: La Beauce is called Beauce precisely because it is not, and *never has been,* flat. A characteristic swelling has always been visible at its centre, forming a sort of outgrowth with bifurcating tips that has stood up to aeons of geological, orogenetic and morphological disturbances and which, from time immemorial, was thought to bring good fortune to those visitors who touched it. In prehistoric times, the distant ancestors of those "carnal" hominids who were to become the Carnalts or Carnutes abandoned their monotonous standing stones in Carnac to make these two "Turres" (the name "Chartres" comes from *Carnutum Turres,* or "Carnutes' Towers") into their special place of pilgrimage and worship.

The Romans, Kyrgyz, Celts, Alans, Basques, Vandals, Vikings, Normans, Occitans and Conquistadores followed in their wake. Such extraordinary popularity, which was to continue unchecked for centuries (and even millennia), explains the proliferation of metamorphoses that Barandard has listed in such thorough and fervent detail. For the *Chartré-dalle* (from the Etruscan *dalle* meaning "stone", as in the modern French *que dalle* (bugger all), or as in Dallas and Dalloz) was primarily and essentially an ecumenical site open to all religious beliefs and practices.

From great invasions to the Front Populaire, from Charles Martel to Charles Péguy, from Charles Trenet to Charles de Gaulle, from NASA to Jean-Paul Chartre, from Hollywood to the Revocation of the Edict of Nantes, from the Night of 4 August to the Three

Glorious Days, from Viollet-le-Duc to the introduction of the TGV, from the Grande-Chartreuse to Marcel Proust, from Chartesian rationalism to the École des Chartes and from the sweeping gesture of the sower of seeds to tourism in *charters*, all of the main historical, ideological and aesthetic currents that have helped to fashion the French spirit have also put their indelible mark on the evolution and development of this site which, along with the Hollow Needle, Versailles, La Samaritaine and the Pompidou Centre, is rightly called one of the gemstones in the crown of universal art.

The question that pre-Romantic artists pondered in their naïve enthusiasm — is the cathedral of Chartres authentic or else purely Romanesque? — has now become irrelevant. Chartres does not have the exclusive rights over any particular style: it is, like Buffon's Man, the epitome of *style* (and even the word "style", from the Greek *style*, or "steeple", is derived from it), so that Renaissance art has its place there just as well as Neo-Moorish, Art Nouveau and the Bauhaus (which is quite simply the German pronunciation of "Beauce").

By turns palaeo-Gothic, archaeozelander, non-Euclidean, proto-Symbolist, Interrealist, hyperclassic, subaquatic (cf. Debussy), post-Raphaelite, pre-Sollersian, quasi-Cubist or crypto-Impressionist, "THE" cathedral of cathedrals rises up in the extraordinary deployment of its different facets as the Essential Manifestation of the Beautiful (or Beauciful). Town-planners, as Barandard so clearly shows, have been quite right to make of Chartres the model for *all* forms of architecture (cf. Le Corbusier, *The Chartres of Athens*), which is equally capable of producing a train terminus or a factory, a town hall or a space station, a detached house or an exhibition centre.

And many have been the poets, from Perrault (*Chartres Beauté*) to Saint-Evremond and from Stendhal (*La Pâmeuse de Chartres*) to Francis Viélé-Griffin, who have allowed us to partake in the incredible exaltation they felt upon discovering what Paul Claudel so beautifully described as "the Priestess of Corn Ears" and which, better than any other, Charles Valéry celebrated as:

> *That tranquil roof where the doves walk*
> *Between the spires the tombs talk*
> *Noon is made of a fire of rain*
> *Corn and more corn rising again*

Georges Perec and Harry Mathews

Roussel and Venice
Outline of a Melancholy Geography

Translated by Antony Melville,
in collaboration with Harry Mathews

Like a flaming comet that holds him fascinated
The astronomer trains his eye observing the canals
(*N. Imp.* 2,75)

In his thesis on turn-of-the-century French playwrights, Mortimer Fleisch[1] devotes a lengthy chapter to Raymond Roussel, and discusses at considerable length five unpublished sheets of paper he was lucky enough to discover and identify in the Fitchwinder University Library. These manuscripts were left to Fitchwinder by Mrs Rosamund Flexner together with three Quarli volumes published in Venice between 1527 and 1540. A note attached to the legacy records that the papers "had been inserted in a cloth pocket between the press-board and the end paper on the recto cover" of a fourth Quarli that is unfortunately lost. The title of this fourth work was *Tragoedia Ducis Partibonis* (The Tragedy of Doge Partibon), printed in Venice in 1532 by Andrea Quarli. It had been bought by Mr Arnold Flexner in Paris in 1936, at a sale where it was advertised as a 16th-century Venetian verse tragedy telling the story of one of the first doges of the "*Città nobilissima e singolare*". The story is somewhat reminiscent of that of Tarquin and Lucretia.[2]

1. Fleisch, M. *Formal Ambiguity in Early Twentieth Century French Theater*, unpublished doctoral dissertation, Carson College, 1975.
2. A second copy of this extremely rare work is to be found in the catalogue of the reserve of the Hermitage Library (Lett. Poj. 2450); a third copy appeared in the

Fleisch's examination of these five pieces of paper[3] led him to suggest that they were the first draft, or rather the outline, of a verse play whose plot, as roughly sketched on the first sheet of paper and presented here in an even more condensed form, was as follows:

The scene is Venice[4] at the end of the 19th century. A young nobleman accused of having assaulted his fiancée is saved at the last minute by two children, the young girl's brother and sister, who had been playing leapfrog on the floor above. Their antics had made the floor shake in such a way as to set free the words the girl had screamed when she was attacked, they had been picked up by the water in the pipes, and fixed in the form of bubbles in the showerhead. The "liquid revelation": "Gob!... Stop!" incriminates

3. See appendix for full texts.
4. Roussel writes V, not Venice, and speaks of a "boatman" rather than a "gondolier". We shall come back to these two points.

auction of the possessions of the Comte de Fortsas on 10 August 1840, with the reference Pat. 55, and the following description: "*Tragoedia Ducis Partibonis*. Venice, Andrea Quarli, 1532, in-folio 10pp. nch., 191 pp. ch. and 1p. nch., rom. char., original binding with wooden boards half bound in brown morocco, vertical design of four rectangles of scrolls with spiral motifs in centre, spine with three ribs decorated with broad criss-cross, three clasps, two of them intact. Painting on fore-edge: the doge is shown in red clothes, speaking to a soldier in armour; his hand is raised in entreaty; the other edges are marbled. Elegant title pages; MS. glosses in a fine humanist hand in margins and on end-papers; some damp-stains to top margin."

Gobbo, the family boatman, who confesses.[5] The girl revives and the marriage is rapidly celebrated.

The first sheet of paper, then, suggests this story, which does not appear at first sight to have been written for the theatre. Sheet 2 shows that we are dealing with a play entitled "In the palace". The four and a half alexandrines on sheet 5 make one inclined to think it is a verse play; one can also deduce from sheets 2 and 5 that one of the characters is called Silvio, probably the unjustly accused fiancé. Sheet 3 is much less easily decipherable; it can at least be clearly seen to be a reference to the insertion of the papers in the Quarli ("inserted into the slit" and "a heavy paper in (as before at the binding)"). Fleisch also makes the relevant point that just as the play is about a rape, the Doge's tragedy tells a story not unlike that of Tarquin and Lucretia. Sheet 4, on the other hand, seems to be indecipherable. Fleisch supposes that it is much earlier than the others (from 1896, with the others much later, sheet 3 in particular being after 1928), but he does not draw any particular conclusions from this, except that Roussel must have returned to this project at several points in the course of his life.

Fleisch makes an obvious mistake at the end of his analysis when he suggests that the theme derives from the transformation of "*la*

5. Sheet 2 reads: "Gobbo, *silent* role" (Roussel's underlining). But he later makes a confession: the significance of this apparent contradiction is made clear later in the article.

vérité sort de la bouche des enfants" [truth comes out of the mouth of children]* into "*la vérité sort de la douche des enfants*" [truth comes out of the children's shower]. The transposition *b/d* is indeed common in Roussel (*le crachat de la bonne à favoris pointus / le crachat de la donne à favoris pointus* [the spit of the maid with fussy suitors / the regalia on the dealt card with pointed side-burns], Dardanelles / *Bard à Nesle* [Dardanelles / bard at Nesle],[6] *la place du bandit sur les tours du fort / la place du dandy sur les tours du fort* [the bandit's place on the towers of the fort / the dandy's bet on the strong man's feats]), but none of the other words here, "truth", "comes out" or "children", conform to Rousselian practice.

The following hypothesis, which follows an equally tried and tested Rousselian procedure, seems more persuasive:

*The nature of Roussel's verbal transformations frequently requires that versions in both languages be given. On such occasions, square brackets are reserved for the English version, round brackets for the French. [Trans.]

6. Cf. *Doc.* 4: Marguerite de Bourgogne conducting a search on the shores of the Black Sea for her bard Slân.

Le viol [the rape]	=	*l'outrage* [the outrage]
une révélation (liquide) [a (liquid) revelation]	=	*est dit* [is spoken]
au moyen d'une douche [by means of a shower]	=	*de douche* [by a shower]
d'une façon intermittente et/ou [intermittently and/or]		
grâce aux sauts des enfants [thanks to the children jumping up and down]	=	*par petits bonds* [in little jumps]
"La Tragédie du Doge Partibon"	=	*L'outrage est dit de douche par petit bonds.*[7]

This was not the first time Roussel had used a title as a starting point (*"Les Ensorcelés du Lac Ontario"* [Bewitched at Lake Ontario], the title of a novel by Gustave Reid which had been a bestseller in 1907, becomes *"Amphore scellées dures a contrario"* [hard sealed amphorae *a contrario*] (*Com.*, 21) and gives rise to the story of the forger Le Marech') but it seemed a good idea in the circumstances to look into the role of this book and in particular the reason for the insertion of the five sheets of paper. It seemed more likely that they were meant to form a whole with the Quarli, although at first sight it was difficult

7. Was there perhaps some corruption — in this case late — of "Doge" into "Duce"? On Roussel's relations with Fascism, see Alvirondi (*Les Écrivains français et la tentation mussolinienne*, third-year thesis, Université de Nice, 1973); the author had access to various state archives.

even to connect them with each other. On this basis, we have taken up the question at the point where Fleisch, who, it must be admitted, had no call to spend more time on it, left off.

The Quarli sold in Paris in 1936 came from the library of a book collector from Lyon, and it has not been possible to establish exactly where it originated (it was presumably sold at public auction, like Roussel's other books and manuscripts, after his death). The most that can be established is that it had formed part of a collection of incunabula and illuminated books assembled in Italy in the early 19th century and dispersed at Turin in 1878.[8] However, while searching for traces of the sale, one of us was able to establish firmly that the *Tragoedia Ducis Partibonis* had been sold a second time in Venice on 17 September 1895.[9]

Now Mme Roussel had at this very sale bought the "Saint John the Baptist" by Groziano which was to be put on sale when Raymond Roussel's collection[10] was dispersed, but which he had withdrawn the day before the sale.[11] It will become clear later in the course of

8. We are particularly grateful to Mme Paulina Petrasova of the Bibliothèque du Tribunal de Commerce for the meticulous research she undertook in auction catalogues.
9. Vianello sale, No. 133; the Palazzo Sarezin archives list it as a "*coll. forestiera*"; there is no mention of an incision in the binding; close study of the description shows that it is not the same copy as the one in the Fortsas sale. (Cf. note 2)
10. Cat. no 19.
11. Letter to M. Baudoin-Dubreuil, dated 6 March 1912. See also Voltic (*Il Museo*

this article why we consider this significant.

Raymond Roussel went to Venice with his mother. He may possibly have been at the sale and bought the Quarli then. It seems more plausible, considering the high prices these items fetch,[12] to suggest that his mother bought it for him, perhaps as a reward for his prize at the Conservatoire.

This stay in Venice, to which, as far as we know, Roussel never referred, lasted about three weeks. The trip was made because Mme Roussel wanted to see one of her childhood friends, Paolina Grifalconi, whom she had met at Friedrichsbad, and who had been recently widowed.[13] [14]

The Grifalconis lived in Venice on the two upper floors of the

12. The last Quarli to be auctioned was sold, as far as we know, in Basel, at Brylinger's, in 1971, for SFr 240,000.

13. Letter to Dr. Reboul, undated (Sept. 95), B.M. Fonds Chambrac, item 843c.

14. It would be improper to make no mention of an eyewitness account which, though it did not give us any major clues, deeply influenced our researches. In the course of a long stay in Venice, one of us recently met an old lady, Mlle Gianna S., who proved to be a distant cousin of the Grifalconis. In the course of a conversation with her, the name Roussel was mentioned, quite by chance; Mlle S.'s reaction was immediate; her face took on an expression of melancholy indignation, while she murmured only the two words *"Povaro Asganio!"* She refused to elaborate.

Immaginario di Roussel, Lo Zecchino, 1976, 3) which interprets the withdrawal as a symptom of Roussel's homosexual urges. The evidence we present later on is, we feel, much more specific about this.

former Palazzo Drasi, on Campo Bragadin, not far from the Mercato delle Fave. The *piano nobile* was let out[15] because Todoro Grifalconi's death had left the family in a rather difficult position financially; this was one of the reasons that had led Mme Roussel to make the trip.

Paolina Grifalconi had two sons: Ascanio, who was then sixteen, and Silvio, who was four. Ascanio was of delicate health, and died the following year on 25 September 1896. Silvio was killed in an accident in 1922 during the riots in Trieste. Mme Grifalconi died in Rome, in 1950, at the age of ninety-three.

We think we can draw the following conclusions from this:

1) it is more than likely that Roussel acquired the Quarli in Venice during the visit he made in 1895;

2) it is highly probable that he was the person who made the incision in the binding;

3) it is not inconceivable that on several separate occasions he slipped into the pocket in the binding papers that concerned in one way or another his memories of Venice and Ascanio.

This is how we propose to explain, though we make no claim to decipher them, the jottings on the fourth sheet of paper, which was

15. At the time of Roussel's trip — they stayed at the Hollenberg — the apartment was let to a young American architect called Joshua Ewett, who was working on the restoration of Santa Maria degli Svevi. In spite of correspondence with his son, Ethan Ewett, of Hartford (Mass.), we have not yet been able to obtain either verbal accounts or documentation about the Grifalconi family.

written in Milan possibly on the very day that Raymond Roussel learned of his young friend's death. "Sep. 95" in any case unquestionably refers to the date of his trip to Venice. The Hôtel de la Plage is, as its name suggests, on the shore of the Adriatic, and it is incidentally well known for its excellent chocolate. The other words remain impenetrable.[16]

It is also, we think, an explanation for the Groziano being withdrawn from sale. This painting, as one of the physical traces of his time in Venice, must not be allowed to pass into the hands of a stranger. Roussel's behaviour over this shows a sort of superstitious piety: he returned the picture to the church of Santa Margherita to which it had originally belonged.[17]

Roussel travelled the length and breadth of Italy several times,

16. "*Singe*" [monkey] could be a rebus-abbreviation of Saint Jean-Baptiste (*singe en batiste* [monkey made of cambric]). "*Crible*" [sieve] reminded us of the "cry" (*cri*) uttered by the girl: "*Gob! Laisse!*" ["Gob! Stop!"]. Could this goblet (*gobelet*) (?) be a mug won by Roussel at the tombola? At this point we are reduced to hypotheses that, spell-binding as they sometimes may seem, are no more than hypotheses. Even though we are deeply convinced that the play, both in its conception *and* in its form, is *bound* to the memory of Venice and Ascanio (it is lodged in the *binding* of the Venetian book), we would be hard put to back up our hunches with straightforward arguments.

17. This church is currently being restored and will not reopen to the public until 1978. We were, however, able to see the picture, which is temporarily housed in the Scuola di San Fantin. A brass plaque screwed on to the lower right-hand corner of the frame declares in French: gift of Mme R. in memoriam A.G., 1912.

but he never returned to Venice. He actually appears to have avoided it by choice. The very name of Venice — and all that Venice automatically conjures up — appears to have been inexorably banished from his works; at the very heart of the Quarli project, the word "gondolier" has been replaced by "boatman".[18]

We think we can explain this silence and Roussel's behaviour in connection with Venice by what is known in psychoanalysis as "incorporation":

Incorporation could thus be defined as a delusion which does all it can to change the world rather than allow the slightest alteration of the subject. It achieves this goal by means of a literal and unshakeable vision of the world. While the process of introjection discovers metaphor and symbol (learning one's mother tongue being the most striking initial instance of this), incorporation stresses the unique, "objective" meaning of words and things, and whenever it encounters metaphorical objects, systematically de-metaphorises them. So when a thing is "hard to

18. We ran through the works looking for explicit references to Italy. There are many less than one might have expected. Most occur in *New Imp.*:

> The Savoyard if when the knell sounds for the pope
> he has to sweep the chimneys clean for the conclave's vote

or
> If in a dream he still has luminous before him
> the idea of his final *allegro*, Tartini

or else
> For a pebble kicked away by any braggart's foot
> the Atlas open at the page with Sicily and Italy

or even
> Andorra, San Marino and even Lichtenstein
> would never provide material for a real book

swallow", it becomes what must be physiologically swallowed: meals and food become obsessions... [The aim of incorporation] is to avoid certain unbearable words ever being spoken. These words are those which are bound up with the loss of the objects of love whose existence was indispensible to the well-being — or quite simply the self-image — of the subject. The object whose loss is denied in this way continues to exist, at the same time as a host of actions, feelings and inexpressible words, in a secret topological system deeply buried in the psyche. Incorporation is therefore a refusal to grieve... Except in the case of delirium or certain kinds of manic-depressive fits, the delusion of incorporation is difficult to diagnose. It is carefully concealed behind masks such as "normality", "character" or "perversion". ... At the melancholic stage, the inner crypt begins to crack and grief is finally accepted. It is unfortunately not felt as the subject's grief for the lost object of love, but as the object's grief for the subject; this is the first psychic modulation, but it is also the last, as it opens the way to surrendering to death.[19]

We apologise for such a long quotation, but a devotee of Roussel can hardly fail to be struck by how well it applies to him, both in his life (periodic obsessions with food and meals, masks of "normality" and "perversion", the Sicilian melancholy of his last journey) and in his work (literality, anti-metaphorism). Incorporation can be generally applied to the overall feeling of Roussel's work: the famous feeling of

19. Pferdli, O., *"Autres images de mélancolie"*, translated from the German by Henri Brunet. *Nouv. Rev. fr. psych.*, 1974, 6.

immobility and immutability which stems from the impression that everything that can happen has already happened, has already been set in place, and which produces a sense of indifference analogous to the numbness one feels at the death of a person one loves, before their death has become an accepted fact or, as Pferdli might have said, before "one has expressed one's grief over it".

A more acute view relating to both his life and his work, though only the second concerns us here, can, we think, be derived from what we have just said: everything Roussel produced suggests an underlying unity which stems neither from "psychology" (which is incapable of describing the work or its development), nor, in spite of its enigmatic characteristics, from a coded hermetic message, which no one wants to decipher any longer anyway. Both in his life and his work, what "changes the world rather than allowing the slightest alteration of the subject" is, to give a banal and literal answer, travel. Roussel was a traveller in real life whose behaviour was often baffling and inscrutable,[20] and a traveller in his writing who strode across vast improbable continents. He went all over the world without seeing it, without looking at it, without being for one moment "impressed" by

20. Virgil Ceaunescu has unearthed an interesting example of such behaviour: a fortnight before going to Bucharest, Roussel wrote to the best stationery printer in the city to order 500 calling-cards headed with the address of the hotel where he was to stay. But he never sent round for them, and did not even stay in that hotel.

it: his "visible" journeys are not the ones to study.

Roussel's work is, we think, a unique commemoration of his other journeys, not the ones he made in his visible life, but those that took place in the "secret topological system" in which he had buried the loss of his one and only object of love: Ascanio. The site of this topography is Venice.

Venice is not the only town to which Roussel never returned, but it is the only one he seems to have forbidden himself to speak of.[21] The absence from his entire work of the city where "imagination and history are inexorably linked", as Pasolo put it so aptly, is surprising in itself, and several researchers have been intrigued by this.

The urban architecture of Venice is pure theatre; it is a *trompe l'oeil* in the context of illusion itself, which can therefore be taken literally: here, deprived of reference to anything outside itself, its reality — which is also Roussel's reality — comes into its own.

Venice is complete and isolated:[22] a whole world, a planet; not only Venus, because of its name, but also Mars, since Venice is red and full of canals. Mars and Venus are the divine, absolute lovers.

21. The comment attributed to Roussel by a journalist on *La Gazette automobile*, "When one arrives in Venice one longs for sweets the size of stars", has been shown to be a brazen forgery by a "hack in need of copy" (unpublished letter from Roussel to Eugène Brigeaud, in *Labyrinthus*, 1974, 1).
22. Isolated: *isole*: Venice is made up of islands. Is it merely coincidence that Roussel should have gone to die on an island, if so many islands appear in his work (Sein, Barbados, Martinique, Reunion, etc.) and *Locus Solus* is an "isolated place"!

Venus was the mother of Aeneas (*Énée*): was Roussel Ascanio's *frère Énée* [*frère aîné* = elder brother]?

Roussel discovered Venice a few months before he was illuminated by his sensation of having extraordinary powers. He discovered there, for the only time in his life, a place that embodied his own sense of reality: the illusion of theatre carved in stone. He went there with his adoring and adored mother. There he met Ascanio, two years younger than him. For the first and only time in his life, we think, a relationship both passionate and tender revealed to him his own desire.

In this sense, Roussel's journey to Venice was his only journey (Venice becomes "Voyage", "Voyage" becomes Venice, and V comes to stand for both Venice and "Voyage"). And like every real journey it was not a departure but a return; he came home, he found his place; it was not an exile but a return to the source, a rediscovery.

Then he left. In the course of the following year, Ascanio died. Venice became the unmentionable place. Thereafter Roussel's life was divided between a social life of "normality" (think of his extreme concern for conventions) and "perversion", which both stem from one mechanical behaviour pattern, and thirty-seven years of a lonely death agony devoted to constructing his "extraordinary travels". Meanwhile, in the depths of his being, he continued to walk with Ascanio through the streets of a Venice that had been banished from the trivial world of his contemporaries, taking refuge in a secret kingdom where the pure and immortal reality of illusion was still alive.

It is not only a verbal coincidence with Pferdli's definition of incorporation that allows us to speak here of a "secret topology": Venice is a city made for walking, where one is never quite sure which way is north or south, where one never knows quite how far it is from one point to another, where the link between two points close together is a question of continuity and/or a break in the surface, just like the space of topology, which disregards direction and scale. Anyone who has spent even a few hours in Venice will have learned how unforeseeable and hard to measure one's movements can be: a street that we think will take us where we want to go brings us back to the *campo* we set out from, a promising thoroughfare ends abruptly at the edge of a stretch of water. These meandering itineraries and the alternation of stone and water, shade and light, turn Venice into the dream space from which Roussel was able to draw the *mappamondo* of his work, the sites and axes of his books, the places and journeys that are the direct projections of the walks and boat-trips he made with Ascanio.

There are then two superimposed topographies in Roussel. One corresponds to the world of his books and generally respects geographical reality (of course there are imaginary towns and countries, but the continents are in the right place); the other is the secret world of his Venetian life. The centre of the first is Paris, the centre of the second the Hollenberg Hotel, where Roussel and his mother stayed. This hotel, which closed in 1915, was unique among the city's grand hotels in that it comprised the Palazzo Hollenberg (now Pasinetti) and a smaller building on the other side of the canal, level with the last big bend before it comes out into the lagoon. The "Paris" equivalent of the canal is the Seine, and the lagoon then plays the part of the Atlantic. Beyond the lagoon lie the beaches of Venice, along the islands which separate it from the Adriatic. Beyond the Atlantic one comes to the Americas: which is, in Roussel, "colonised" (Guyana) just as the beaches are *"colonies d'été"* [summer colonies] for the Venetians. To the south, in both cases, one crosses stretches of water, the Mediterranean and the Great Canal, to "unknown" lands: Africa and the group of islands which, in 1895, were still almost unbuilt on.

It is immediately obvious that these topographies are mirror images of each other: America is west of Paris, while the beaches are east of Venice. This "real" geographical fact is not an explanation. We find it much more relevant to point out that to someone for whom illusion is the very stuff of reality, something seen in a mirror is infinitely more real than the supposedly real objects that give rise to the reflection. The reversal of spatial organisation in Roussel's two worlds is therefore the key to this topological equivalence, whose emblem is Roussel's own monogram.

On the basis of this general outline, as shown in the diagram

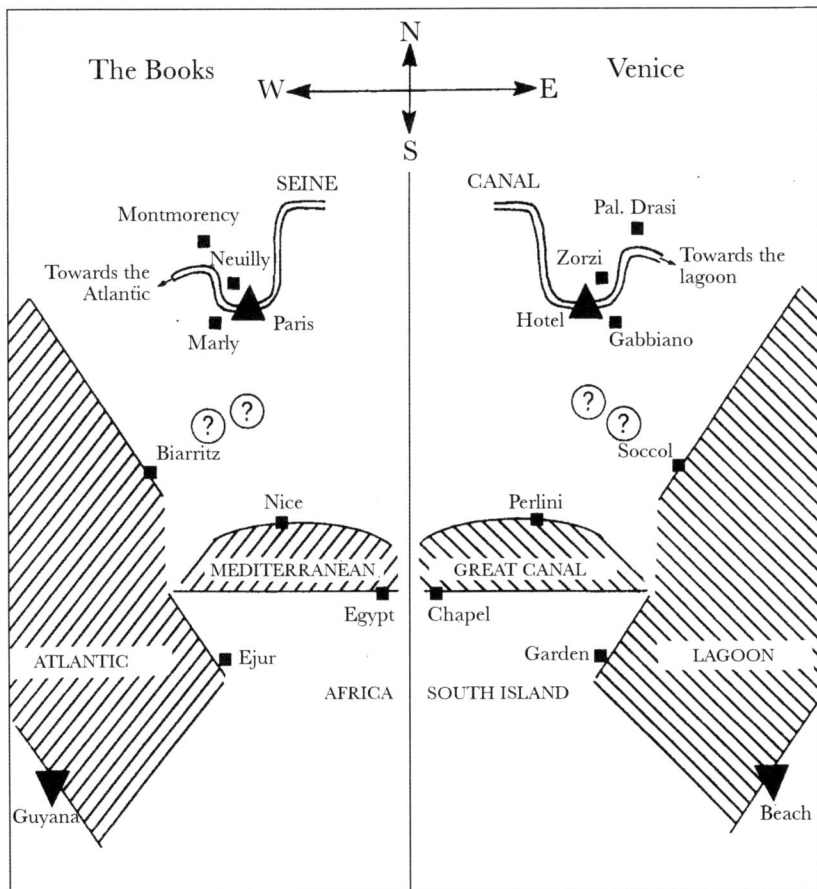

The Books | Venice

N
W ← → E
S

The Books:
- SEINE
- Montmorency
- Neuilly
- Towards the Atlantic
- Paris
- Marly
- ? ?
- Biarritz
- Nice
- MEDITERRANEAN
- Egypt
- ATLANTIC
- Ejur
- AFRICA
- Guyana

Venice:
- CANAL
- Pal. Drasi
- Zorzi
- Towards the lagoon
- Hotel
- Gabbiano
- ? ?
- Soccol
- Perlini
- GREAT CANAL
- Chapel
- Garden
- LAGOON
- SOUTH ISLAND
- Beach

above, one can try to imagine a point-for-point correspondence between the topography in the books and the course of the Venetian love affair that can be read behind the convolutions of the major works.[23]

23. The hypotheses we put forward about these correspondences are based on a systematic analysis of guides to Venice published at the turn of the century, especially the Zanotti.

LA DOUBLURE [The Lining*]: Paris-Nice — "and the whole Côte d'Azur" — Neuilly

Paris, as we have seen, is the Hollenberg Hotel. The Cote d'Azur could be the bank of the Great Canal (the "European" side) — a particularly promising analogy in that this is one of the Venetians' favourite walks in the winter months. Nice would then be the celebrated Caffé Perlini, which was famous in the winter for its *gatto caldo* (a sort of boiling-hot punch) and in summer for its sorbets. It is hard to imagine a tourist spending three weeks in Venice without going to the Perlini at least once, and it was probably one of the first fashionable spots to which Ascanio would have wanted to introduce Roussel. As for Neuilly, a place which is "near the centre", north of the river (the canal), its Venetian equivalent would be between the Hollenberg and the Palazzo Drasi (where the Grifalconis lived): for instance Da Zorzi, on the Campo San Domenico, a tea room that was very fashionable at the time, where Ascanio and Roussel would have been able to meet their mothers at the end of one of their walks.

LA VUE [The View]: Biarritz (?) — A grand hotel — A spa

Whether or not the seaside resort described in the first poem is Biarritz (as is generally supposed), it is unquestionably on the Atlantic coast, and therefore, in the Venetian version, on the lagoon; it could

* "*La Doublure*" also means "The Understudy". [Trans.]

be, for instance, the extension of the great square which comes down to the waterfront. This is where, in the '90s, an enterprising restaurateur named Gustavo Soccol started an open-air restaurant, a sort of smart precursor of modern snack bars. Young Venetians were very partial to his light, hot meals, and it is by no means implausible to suggest that Ascanio and Roussel lunched there together.

Since the other two poems are much less specifically sited geographically, it is more difficult to deduce their Venetian correspondences with any precision. Possibly the descending progression of areas of water in the three parts of the book — ocean, lake, and pond — is significant; in which case the two other scenes must be further "inland". Given that the equivalent of a grand hotel and a spa could be one of the luxury establishments Roussel adored, we can suggest two, both within the perimeter of high-class shops which line the square on the inland side: the famous tailor Bordino's, or the hair salon where the famous Roncali plied his trade.

IMPRESSIONS D'AFRIQUE [Impressions of Africa]: Near the west Coast of Africa, not far from Porto Novo

The passengers on the *Lyncée* cross the Mediterranean and part of the Atlantic before they are washed up on the black continent: Ascanio and Roussel cross the Great Canal, round the tip of the South Island through a narrow passage, and land on its East coast. This part of Venice was very different then from what it is now: there were gardens, orchards and fields, a rustic landscape full of trees and exotic flowers, an almost wild smell. Anne d'Azay, who visited the island in 1897, wrote: "I half expected monkeys to appear among the trees; I was almost scared to walk into the warm shade of the thickets."

One need not go so far as to suggest that Ascanio and Roussel actually lay down side by side in this warm shade, but one can easily believe that in this luxuriant, *unfamiliar world* so close to the civilised delirium of the Venetian palazzi, Roussel discovered the erotic power of his passion. He may have found it a dark force which knocked him off course, just as the passengers of the *Lyncée* while off course discovered Africa against their will (it is worth noting in this context that the words "vessel" and "canal" can, in anatomy for instance, be synonymous). In any case, he made this place his "Inner Africa", the dark, nocturnal continent of his desire.[24]

LOCUS SOLUS: Montmorency

Montmorency is a few miles northwest of Paris; the Palazzo Drasi is a few hundred yards northeast of the Hollenberg Hotel. Could any place be more deserving of the name "Locus Solus" than Ascanio's house? In this sense "Solus" obviously means "unique", a

---

24. It is worth pointing out that the *Lyncée* was *en route* for South America, but none of the passengers reached this destination.

meaning which the book and its brilliant protagonist constantly bring to mind, but which Roussel took care to formally disclaim in the opening lines of the first chapter.

It is also in *Locus Solus* that the process of turning the world to stone is most clearly apparent: the entire novel is a walk past "monuments in action", frozen commemorations looked upon by anonymous faceless people who could just as easily be ghosts.

L'ÉTOILE AU FRONT [The Star on the Forehead]: Marly-Paris

Marly is a wealthy residential suburb to the south of Paris. In the "Venetian mirror" it could be for instance Il Gabbiano ingabbiato, a restaurant deservedly famous for its fish and seafood (it is still in existence but nothing remains to suggest its former glory). The establishment's "class" would suggest a dinner outing with the Grifalconis and the Roussels "*en famille*", after which Roussel would have walked with his mother back to the Hollenberg round the corner.

LA POUSSIÈRE DE SOLEILS [Dust of Suns]: Guyana

The other side of the Atlantic, that is, the lagoon, is the bathing beach, the Venetians' Eden during their warm Septembers, where one can easily imagine that Ascanio and Roussel went swimming together.

In our discussion of *Impressions* we pointed out that the

passengers of the *Lyncée* never reached the Americas, their original destination. Here we are at last in the "New World". Though we have rigorously refrained from discussing circumstantial, unquantifiable, and in Roussel's case obviously ambiguous correspondences between his writing and his experience in Venice, we cannot omit the observation that *Poussière* describes a treasure hunt that ends with the treasure being found: was Roussel's passion, perhaps, physically consummated on the beach? Or perhaps not "on the beach" (bathing arrangements in 1895 did not on the whole facilitate such things), but "at the Hôtel de la Plage" which Roussel refers to on sheet 4, or back in Venice, at the Palazzo Drasi, since the play whose fragments we have rediscovered appears to have been entitled "In the Palace" (cf. sheet 2). This final play, the projected apex of Roussel's work, would then be a commemoration of the event; but it is more realistic to suggest that just as the play got no further than a barely sketched outline, their physical love remained at the stage of passionate promises,[25] and the "treasure" they found was in fact the discovery that their love was mutual.

---

25. In *Poussière*, it should be pointed out, however, the words *Lit de haut* appear twice, and mention is made of a *Lie d'O*. [upper bed, dregs of O].

LES NOUVELLES IMPRESSIONS D'AFRIQUE [New Impressions of Africa]: Egypt: Damietta — The Pyramids — Damietta area — Outside Cairo

We return to Africa. Not "black" Africa this time, but the place of the dead, of mummies and tombs. Its mirror image, at the western end of "Venetian Africa", could be the wonderful baroque chapel of Santa Cecilia, where lovers are said traditionally to come to exchange vows. We cannot resist thinking that in choosing Egypt to commemorate this last outing with Ascanio, Roussel became painfully aware of the wretched irony of the love he had borne all his life: the sanctuary he had built contained only the dead body of Ascanio. The discovery set the seal on his unhappiness.

We can now return to the five sheets of paper whose physical history we think we have reconstructed, and whose meaning we would now like to look at further in the light of the last few paragraphs.

The "incorporated" memory of Ascanio, inscribed in an incision in a precious book, like a wound that will never close, fuelled an impossible work which was the total book Roussel dreamed of all his life: the book that would bring him recognition from all quarters, the book that would be a poem, the poem that would be a play — a book and a play in *trompe l'œil*.

The relationship between the play and Ascanio (sheet 4) belongs to Roussel's secret equations, and the project is not developed far enough for one to hazard a guess at it. All one can deduce is that the fiancé character was originally called Ascanio, and the name was then changed to Silvio (cf. sheet 2: "Asc is called Silvio"), so that the second line of the couplet on sheet 5, "*Ramener Silvio sur le lieu du forfait*" [To take back Silvio to the scene of the crime], does not scan unless one pronounces it Sil-vi-o, so that one is strongly tempted to read it as "*Ramener Ascanio [As-ca-nio] sur le lieu du forfait*" [To take back Ascanio to the scene of the crime]. From there onwards, as we have said (note 16), one can only indulge in deliberate speculation.

One can see more clearly how the Quarli is pivotal to the project. Sheet 2 is particularly clear about this. The basic descriptive characteristics of the Quarli seem to have been used, under one of Roussel's usual procedures, to form the constituent parts of the play:

travail de vers (de livre) [(book) worm-eaten]	=	*livre (pièce) travaillée en vers* [book (play) written in verse]
mouillures [damp stains]	=	*gouttes d'eau* [drops of water]
dos à nerfs [ribbed spine]	=	? *(punition de Gobbo)* [? (punishment of Gobbo)]
*a fondello*26 [*a fondello*]	=	*révélation qui vient du "fond de l'eau"* [revelation coming "from the depths"]
fermoir [clasp of book, or tap of shower]	=	*(douche)* [(shower)]

26. The parchment covers, before the binding was done, bore one of the following

The clasp (*fermoir*) is the thing that closes, that seals, thus conceals, and that does not speak ["shut up!" (in French *"la ferme!"*)]; the shower/(mouth) (*douche/ (bouche)),* is what holds back the water (*l'eau*), what holds back the confession (*l'aveu*): what cannot speak the impossible word. Given that it is actually put in brackets, we find this the strongest possible image of "incorporation": the truth is inscribed (inserted) in the book, but the book is closed; it will say nothing (Gobbo confesses but remains *silent*).

tranches (peintes) [(painted) edges] = *(texte) en tranches* [(text) in sections]

As always in Roussel, words have to be taken in their strict meaning. When Roussel associates the clasp with a shower, he has in mind the physical image of a book whose clasp resembles a shower attachment. When he refers to a text in sections, he has in mind a text that can be physically separated into sections. Again, when he adds, lower down, after listing the roles in the play: *"chacun représentant un rôle"* [each representing a role], which would appear to be superfluous, this can only mean that the word "role" does not here refer to the *"dramatis personae"* but to its etymological root — the rolls of paper on which actors' texts were written.

two hand-written inscriptions: *coverto*, if it was to be a full binding, or *a fondello*, if it was a half-binding (Beaujeu and Petitjean, *Histoire du Livre*, Paris, 1960).

Our final hunch, based on the foregoing and on a difficult reading of sheet 3, is that Roussel had in mind for his play a single stage apparatus for use in a performance in which he would mime *all the roles/rolls*, drawing them ("casting" them to himself) out of a book as it was broken into sections that would form the set (*tranches peintes* = painted sections).[27]

"The book which on one side only arrests the eye and masks" would then be a replica (all plays are made of "*répliques*" [= replies, replicas]) of the Quarli, a *trompe-l'oeil* book made of wood with sections that might be painted with the principal scenes of the play, and a clasp carved in the form of a showerhead. It would open up to reveal "rolls" which Roussel would take out and read one after another ("*à tour de rôle*").

This is not the first time[28] that Roussel refers to a "book with a secret", or a "binding with a pocket". But, just as in the Frascati episode, the "precise apparatus" refers both to the spring mechanism

---

27. This idea may date from the late period when Roussel was a ruined man, but still addicted to the theatre, and thought of putting to use the talents as a mime, musician and actor which had given him his greatest society successes.

28. "Having once again been called a '*Sénéchal*' by Frascati, the 'fence' had straight away to insert his nail into the delicate graining of the parchment [...] Which unknown to him set off the precise mechanism the Genoan had placed there. The binding opened, to reveal the three letters which saved the numismatist" (*Imp.* 147).

ordered from Bordaz the clock-maker, which has been described in detail four pages before, and to the whole mechanism devised to confuse Neyric the receiver, this play when read "as an open book", through the moving brevity of the five surviving sheets of paper, stands at the same time for the final silence of the text and the "coming apart" on which it is based. The "precise apparatus" in fact made Roussel incapable throughout his life of undertaking this play, which was to declare the dislocated scene of his desire and the actual figure of his "renaissance": the Renaissance book (the Quarli), and the renaissance (resuscitation) of Sibylla, who comes back to life to celebrate her marriage to Ascanio/Silvio, will remain forever still-born.

One cannot expect the exegesis of a few lines, however assiduously one may have dissected them from every possible angle, to cast much light on a body of work that was so well described in the words of Bachter as "a literary adventure having no source but itself, no end except its own existence, and no other meaning than the trail it leaves".[29]

It is ultimately of no importance whether one can discover, running through these paltry fragments, the thread of a project on which Roussel might have laboured all his writing life with a view to making it his crowning work, the "masterwork" that would have won

29. Bachter, B.O., "*Les Lieux solitaires*", *Bull. Inst. Ling. Louvain*, 1972, 97: 103-14.

him general recognition. There is no Roussel mystery; his work is not a riddle that we must solve. It is only our reading of it, our thirst for explanation, our love of complexity that creates the impression that there is a secret to be cracked. If secret there is, it will not be found where we look for it.[30]

Any attempt to explain Roussel stumbles over the obstinate fact of his unfathomable method. Our claim that the hypothetical play whose possible origins we have attempted to describe is the last, posthumous metonym of a trip to Venice around which the delusion of writing was organised derives not from any illusion that our arguments define Roussel but, in the last resort, from the incomparably Roussellian emotion the traveller feels when, standing on the steps of the Evangelisti, he discovers for the first time the city of which Roussel was the mental architect.

October 1975-December 1976

---

30. Nothing could be simpler, for instance, than to explain the ballerina's costume in the episode of the lawyer Dargaud (*LS* 176) by means of a near pun on "*Meunier, tu dors*" [Miller, you are sleeping] ("*Manille et Tudor*": *manille* [anklet] referring to the hoop with which the dancer's crinoline is made, and *Tudor* to the roses on her bodice); but the whole episode could just as easily be linked to the slang expression "*Je n'ai pas un rotin*" [I haven't a bean] which becomes "*jeune épouse à rotin*" [young wife with hoops]: both expressions are equally valid, equally stimulating, and equally useless.

In a few years' time, the entire work of Roussel will have been computerised and subjected to a statistical analysis of self-correlations and cross-correlations that will make it possible to define systematically all the significant variations affecting his vocabulary, syntax, metrics, and even semantics (frequency of half-words, obligatory associations, etc.). So we hear at any rate from Prof. Vance de Gregorio, director of this project at the Parnell Institute for Advanced Research. The results of this analysis will no doubt confirm and clarify what we already know. It is doubtful whether they will enable us to learn anything about things Roussel himself did not allow us to glimpse. The taste for riddles, though not enough by itself, is in this case a better tool than the most powerful computer.

Sheet 1

At the end of the last century a prominent family lived in V, called the Z, whose daughter, Sib, was engaged to a young nobleman.

The engagement period was nearly ended, when, after a visit by   to the Palazzo   , the governess found Sib unconscious in the luxurious bathroom that adjoined her room. The young girl held clenched in her hand a batiste handkerchief embroidered with the initials of her fiancé, who was immediately accused of having assaulted her.

The evidence was overwhelming since no one had seen the young man come out after going with Sib into the music room where she usually spent the afternoon.

        was arrested and taken to the court-house where an attempt was made to reconstruct this base assault.

Soon everyone was gathered in the young girl's room except the two youngest Z children, a boy and a girl who were playing *leap-frog* in the huge attics of the Palazzo.

At this point the young girl's voice was heard coming from the bathroom, in distant, intermittent, but perfectly audible snatches, pronouncing the inexorable accusation that revealed the truth about this horrible crime: GOB!... STOP!

There could be no doubt about the meaning of these words, which pointed to Gobbo, the hunchbacked boatman to the family, who was promptly questioned and soon admitted his guilt.

Sib's shouts had been intercepted by the water in the pipes and held in the shower-head attached above the bath.

The children had in the course of their innocent games caused the shower attachment to shake in a particular way that released the fateful words.

Sib, when to everyone's surprise she emerged from the coma the assault had induced, confirmed this curious liquid revelation.

No time was lost in celebrating, on the water, a sumptuous wedding in which the two youngest children were given the place of honour they thoroughly deserved.

In the Palazzo

Asc is called Silvio

Worm eaten

damp stains

ribbed spine   .

a fondello

clasp   (shower)

painted edges

book in sections

casting of roles   the father

the mother

Silvio

Sib

Govern

Gobbo the hunchback, *silent* role

the two children

each corresponding to one role

Sheet 3

far here. 20 vol

instalment

folded both sides

    and because of that

    addition of one

sheet in the opposite direction

inserted, into the slit   against

death

renaissance?

for +

one never finds

a role that goes the

other way

— there is another sheet

to cater for the possibility

of this other way

series of roles

the book that from only one side   gilding —

— arrests the eye —   a heavy paper

and masks   in (as before

at the binding)

Sheet 4

(on headed notepaper from the GRANDE ALBERGO DEI PRINCIPI DI MALTA Via San Cosimo degli Incurabili, 14, Milano)

chocolate

At the *de la Plage*

Sep 95

the ivory of his

sieve

monkey

tombola (SM)

red

Handkerchief

By overcoming his nerves he will be able thus

To take back Silvio to the scene of the crime

As to the erect purple of the clasp which an oaf...

There could be no purer oath to give to you

BOOKS OF RELATED INTEREST FROM ATLAS PRESS

THE OULIPO *Winter Journeys*

CONTENTS:
Georges Perec *Le Voyage d'hiver: The Winter Journey*
Jacques Roubaud *Le Voyage d'hier: Yesterday's Journey*
Hervé le Tellier *Voyage d'Hitler: Hitler's Journey*
Jacques Jouet *Hinterreise*
Ian Monk *Le Voyage d'Hoover: Hoover's Journey*
Jacques Bens *Le Voyage d'Arvers: Arvers's Journey*
Michelle Grangaud *Un Voyage divergent: A Divergent Journey*
François Caradec *Le Voyage du ver: The Worm's Journey*
Reine Haugure *Le Voyage du vers: Verse's Journey*
Harry Mathews *Le Voyage des verres: A Journey Amidst Glasses*

Harry Mathews & Alastair Brotchie (eds.) *Oulipo Compendium*

Harry Mathews *The Way Home, Collected Longer Prose*

For more details see our website:

www.atlaspress.co.uk